FASCINATION

SHIFTERS FOREVER AFTER

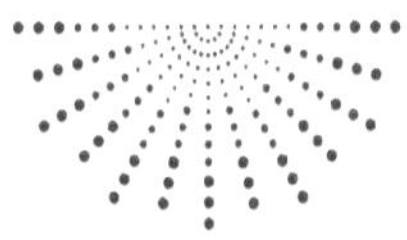

ELLE THORNE

Thank you for reading!

*To receive exclusive updates from Elle Thorne and to be the
first to get your hands on the next release,
please sign up for her newsletter.
Put this in your browser:
ellethorne.com*

Book 2 of Shifters Forever After: A spin off series of Shifters Forever.

Black panther shifter Cadence Araya, sexy, curvy, and edgy. She knows what she's doing is wrong—ish. But why she's doing it is quite right. Hopefully she's not caught before she reaches her goal.

Polar bear shifter Isaac Romanoff's been selected to serve on a special Task Force investigating a string of burglaries committed by a very talented cat burglar. The elusive thief has evaded capture for a couple of years. He suspects the criminal is a shifter.

He's in for a hell of a surprise.

Enjoy!

Elle Thorne Newsletter

If you can't click, just put this in your browser:
http://www.ellethorne.com/news.html

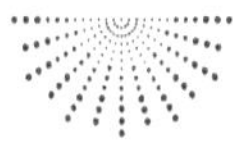

*N*o one said being a cat burglar would be easy.

But it was worth it. And it was the quickest way for black panther shifter Cadence Araya to get her hands on a boatload of money.

Eyes burning like she'd had a handful of sand thrown in them, Cade was suffering from a sleepless night, but she couldn't pass up this dinner. She hadn't seen her sister Laken in a month, not since she'd left for Africa to work with the victims of war. She'd taken her new mate Ky Romanoff with her. He'd given up a prestigious job with the Shifter Supreme Court to travel with Laken, and they were coming back today.

Cade missed Laken. Missed her sister's caring mannerisms. Missed the way she calmed her when Cade was in a tizzy over the details of one job or another. Except Laken didn't know about Cade's jobs.

Miss Goody Two Shoes that she was, Laken wouldn't get it.

Nope, not one bit.

"Ready?" Cade turned to their baby sister Carina.

"What's the hurry? We're not expected for another hour." Cari yanked on the zipper on her pants. The zipper's steel teeth sealed with a metal-on-metal grinding sound. The two sisters were meeting Laken and Ky at the Romanoffs—Ky's aunt and uncle—for dinner.

"I don't know. I'm just antsy." Cade tugged on her dress's hem. She hated dresses; she'd rather be in her yoga pants and a comfy tee that hugged her curves just so.

"Because of last night's job? I thought you said it went okay."

I lied. "It did."

Of course Carina knew about Cade's nighttime activities. Cade had to confess after Cari found Cade's stash of equipment. Not a very abundant stash, but when one considered what else was in the stash— jewels and cash, lots of it—Carina had a right to ask questions.

And Cade couldn't lie to her.

So she'd told Cari everything—including what she was doing with the money.

Cari understood, but that didn't stop her from

worrying and hovering like an overprotective hen at times.

"Let's get a latte on the way. My treat."

CADE AND CARI arrived early at the Romanoff resi-dence. Ky's uncle Mikhail and aunt Miriam were welcoming and sweet, making them feel comfortable.

Laken and Ky were a few minutes behind. A luggage situation, Miriam explained.

They'd just become acquainted with the Romanoffs and Ky's brother Jonah, a polar bear shifter, when a knock sounded at the door.

Miriam slipped away to open it. Seconds later, Cade heard the deep timbre of Ky's voice, and the softer sound of Laken's.

Then she heard Miriam say, "I've never seen you so happy. Come in. Almost everyone's here. Including Carina and Cadence. And they've missed you."

"Almost everyone?" Ky's voice. "Let me guess, Jonah's not here."

Miriam laughed. "Oh, no. He's here. This time it's your other brother Isaac. He said he'd be a few minutes late. Something to do with a case."

"Did Mae and the others make it safely to Bear Canyon Valley?" Ky again.

"No incidents, thankfully," Miriam said. "And we've seen Bain twice. He had lunch with your uncle once, and dinner with both of us last week."

Cari tugged on Cade's sleeve and they headed for the front door. They grabbed Laken in a hug.

"I'm glad you're home." Cari took Laken's hand. "Tell me you're staying through the holidays."

"Yes, say you are," Cade insisted.

Miriam shuttled them toward the next room.

Mikhail came in, carrying three wine glasses filled with dark red wine. He handed Laken, Cade, and Carina a glass each. "Merlot? You'll love this one, if you're a fan. It's a special edition."

"Thank you," Laken said to Mikhail, accepting the wine glass. "And yes, we're staying through the holidays. What have you two been up to?"

"Just work," Cari said.

"You?" Laken looked at Cade.

Cade shrugged. *Oh, just a burglary or two.* "Work, mostly." She took a sip of the wine.

Behind them came the sound of a door opening.

"Isaac!" Miriam hastened away and hugged a large polar bear shifter. "You made it."

Cade's attention was riveted on the newcomer. Square jaw, chiseled features, eyes the color of the ocean in Cozumel, the place she and Carina had vacationed a little over a month ago. Laken had bought tickets for all three, but she'd had to bail and serve on the Shifter Supreme Court.

Cade harnessed her mind, bringing her wandering thoughts back to the present. She also averted her eyes, lest she be caught staring.

Though he was easy to stare at. A fascinating combination of sapphire eyes, dark brown hair, and stubble in dire need of a razor emphasized the man's innate sexiness.

A pair of dark circles under his eyes made her think of her own artfully covered signs of sleeplessness. She'd laid the concealer on heavy today.

He glanced away from his aunt, his posture on guard, his gaze surveying and taking reconnaissance. His scrutiny over Cari was a quick glance, then he did the same to Cade.

No. Not exactly. There was no such thing as a quick glance when it came to Cadence Araya.

His eyes traveled from hers and down her body, then back up again, and settled on her eyes.

The depths of his sapphire gaze had a gold flicker. She recognized his bear. Then to her dismay, Cade's panther growled in her mind, making assertions that Cade wasn't interested in and didn't have time for. She pushed her panther back, not allowing her a voice. Her panther snarled, and this time the snarl was pure frustration aimed directly at Cade.

Isaac Romanoff… She ran the name through her

mind, savoring it. She couldn't pull her eyes from his face.

"How's the case?" Ky asked Isaac after the two brothers had hugged.

Isaac's gaze tore from hers and he turned his attention to his brother. "Goddamned cat burglar. Things escalated shortly after you left. But I think we may be getting close."

"What?" Carina glanced at Isaac, then at Cade, then back to Isaac, a guilty look on her face.

Jesus. Don't react to that word.

She'd have to remind Cari to be a little more poker-faced and not let people see that the words "cat burglar" caught her attention. She nudged Cari.

His scent, manly with a hint of the outdoors, infiltrated her senses, filling her lungs. She breathed out, fighting to regain control over her senses. "I'm Cadence."

Cari took her cue. "I'm Laken's sister. Carina. Cari, preferably."

"Isaac." He shook Cari's hand, but his eyes were glued on Cade.

The intensity of his gaze made her pulse pick up speed.

"What's this about a cat burglar?" Cari asked with an almost full-blown telltale glance at Cade.

Cade ground her teeth in frustration. *Keep it up, little*

sister. They'll have me serving several sentences at this rate. Carina was practically announcing Cade's guilt.

Miriam beamed with pride. "Isaac's with the NYPD. He's a detective. Let's go into the living room. We've got appetizers galore."

"Special Task Force," Ky added.

"Quit that, you two." The sex-on-a-stick any woman would've liked to lick shook his head, then turned to Cari. "I've been assigned to the cat burglar case."

Cade bit back a gasp, digging sharp teeth into her bottom lip.

"You said you were getting close?" Cari probed.

For the love of all that's holy, shut the fuck up, Carina. Cade forced a smile to her face, hoping that was what she'd plastered there, but unsure, because damn, her face felt like it was in a grimace from hell.

"Do you still think it's a shifter?" Ky asked.

It happened. Cade had no control over it. It was like her fingers stopped functioning the second that question left Ky's lips.

Her glass plummeted to the Italian tile, shattering into a myriad of tiny, sparkling, catch-the-light pieces that teased Cade with how much they reminded her of diamonds. The tiny shards that had wine on them reminded her of rubies.

Or blood.

Yeah, mine. Blood's going to be shed because Laken's going to kill me if she finds out what I've been up to.

A shiver prickled its way down her spine while her face's temperature dropped.

My crimes returning to haunt me.

Cade looked up from the mess on the floor. "Sorry," she whispered. "I don't know what happened."

Miriam patted her on the shoulder. "Don't concern yourself. It's an easy fix. I'll be right back."

Isaac's eyes narrowed.

Cade cringed at what that could mean. *Or maybe it means nothing and I'm too damned paranoid.*

What were the fucking odds that the brother of her sister's mate would be the one hunting her down?

I should stop now.

"Let me help." Cade trailed Miriam toward the kitchen.

I should stop before my tush is busted.

Miriam opened a drawer in the kitchen and handed Cade a handful of paper towels. She reached into the large pantry and pulled out a cordless mini-vacuum cleaner.

"I wish you'd let me clean it up," Miriam said, her eyes traveling over Cade's face. "You don't look well."

Great. I look a mess when the only man I've been attracted to in ages is here. Figures. Not to mention he wants me in cuffs, and not the sexy, fuzzy kind.

What the hell was she thinking? She couldn't be

attracted to him. His mission was to see her behind bars.

I've lost it. It's official.

From the other room, she heard Isaac's voice. "Is she okay?"

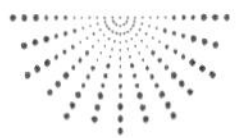

D*amn.*

That was the first thought that came to Isaac's mind when he saw Cadence Araya.

The second thing that entered his mind was his bear, in terms of decibel level. His bear completely lost it, roaring and growling, creating a ruckus in Isaac's mind that made it difficult to concentrate on anything else.

She was stunning. A beauty, but not of the conventional type. Eyes so dark they were unfathomable, gleaming with a spirit that intrigued him, fascinated him. Her cheekbones looked as if they'd been sculpted by an artist, and her figure… it was lush and gorgeous, curves on top of curves.

A throb in his pants cautioned an impending disaster if he didn't rein in his thoughts.

Down, fella, he cautioned his bear, as if this was all his bear and only his bear, and had nothing to do with Isaac himself.

No, nothing at all. Not one bit.

Denial wouldn't serve him; he knew that.

One second he was getting ribbed by his family, then Ky asked him a question… something… Isaac was hard pressed to remember what, because his mind was focused on Cadence.

Then a second later, she was pale, her glass shattered on the floor, her light gray pants speckled with wine.

Jonah slipped into the room. "I have to go."

"Before dinner?" Aunt Miriam didn't hide her disappointment, pouting. "You haven't had dinner with us for a while. What's up, Jonah? Is there something you're not telling us?"

Isaac could see something was going on with Jonah, but he was half-distracted by that fascinating creature with the obsidian eyes. Jonah would share whatever it was when he was ready. Isaac wasn't about to pry, and he knew Ky wouldn't, either.

"I'll try to come by some evening this week, Aunt Miriam." Jonah strode toward the front door.

"That's what you said last time."

"I promise." Jonah's voice trailed behind him.

Isaac turned toward Cadence and his aunt.

"Take Cadence into the dining room," his aunt said. "She doesn't look well."

Shit, I think she looks great. But he knew what his aunt meant. Cadence didn't really look like she was okay. Her color had gone from pale cream to a light tint of Frankenstein green.

Isaac put his hand behind her back to guide her.

He didn't expect she'd flinch when he touched her back. He also didn't expect the surge of energy that traveled through him, even though their flesh was separated by the fabric of her clothing.

Was that what she was reacting to? He inhaled deeply, hoping her scent would give her emotions away.

Nothing.

Nothing? How could it be? Block? Why was she using hunter's block? No shifter did that unless they wanted to hide something.

His cop mentality took over, suspicious and curious about what she could want to hide.

What secrets are you keeping, little panther?

ISAAC SPENT the rest of the evening concentrating on Carina, because she seemed like a safer bet than trying to manage a coherent thought process around

Cadence. His bear's constant rampage and range of emotions had Isaac's mind roaring and going in circles.

Dinner took forever and at the same time seemed to last less than a moment. Forever because it was hellishly difficult not to look at the curvy brunette. And less than a moment because he wanted to spend the rest of eternity with her.

Nah, hell no, I didn't just go there.

His bear growled assent. He sure as hell had gone there.

I have no business getting emotionally involved with a woman. Didn't I learn my fucking lesson well enough last time?

His last relationship had not ended well.

Understatement of the year, that's for sure.

His bear rumbled.

Yeah, we won't go there.

"How was Africa?" he asked Ky.

"Hot. Rewarding. We're going to the Middle East next."

"I didn't think you'd ever go back there."

"Different cause, different purpose. Different traveling companion." Ky put his arm around Laken. She leaned into his shoulder.

His brother Ky had served in the Middle East with Sigma Eps, the paranormal unit of the special forces.

"Very different traveling companion, no doubt. Much prettier," Isaac agreed.

Laken blushed, the light pink color kissing her cheeks. "Stop it or we'll start talking about your Special Task Force."

He raised his napkin, waving it in surrender. "I give."

He liked his brother's mate. Straightforward and sweet. What a contrast to the darkness he saw in Cadence. Not a bad darkness, a mysterious one. A darkness he liked, one he wanted to explore.

"I know what!" Laken grinned. "Come over tomorrow night. My place. Cade and Cari will be there. A family gathering."

The only thoughts he had of Cadence didn't have anything to do with family.

Across from Laken, Cadence choked, coughing and spurting, her face turning red while Carina pounded on her back.

Cadence turned to her. "That doesn't help," she exclaimed, trying to breathe between bites. She raised a glass of water to her lips and drank sips between coughing fits.

"I hope that doesn't mean you don't like the Salisbury steak," Miriam said, then added, "This just doesn't seem to be a good night for you, dear."

"Sure doesn't seem like it," Cadence wheezed.

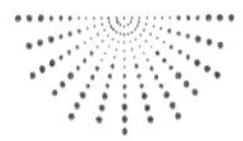

"That could not have gone any more horribly if my worst enemy had planned it." Cade tossed her purse onto the bed and leaned her forehead against the wall.

"It sucked. It totally sucked."

Of course it did. The first guy she'd been attracted to in a long time and…

One, he's a fucking cop and he's hunting me.

Two, he thinks I'm a coughing, klutzy mess.

Three… shit. Give me time. I'll come up with three. And by the time I do, there'll probably be a dozen more to add to that list.

A knock at the door brought her forehead off the wall.

"Cade?"

She ground her teeth. She was still a touch peeved with Cari.

I mean, jeez, could she have been more obvious?

"Yeah."

Carina opened the door. "I'm really sorry about tonight. I got spooked."

You pretty much put a neon sign over my head that said Cadence the Cat Burglar.

She couldn't say that to Cari. She just couldn't. It would crush her little sister.

But I'll have to quit or move. I can't have such a glaring trail leading to my actions.

Then again, she wasn't far from reaching her goal. Just a couple more jobs.

At what risk?

Cade pushed that thought away. It wouldn't serve her to think that way. She wrapped her arms around Cari. "Don't worry. Just be more careful, okay?"

Cari nodded. Her dark eyes, so similar to Cade's and Laken's, were full of tears. "I'm going to avoid him."

"You can't avoid him. We're expected at Laken's tomorrow night." *Oh, hell no, I'm not going alone. That's too damned close to a double date.*

"I've already decided." Cari's jaw jutted forward in stubbornness. When she wore that look, there was no changing her mind.

Time to appeal to Cari's love for their sister. "Laken will be disappointed."

"She'll be fine. I'll offer to take her to lunch the day after."

Ugh. Why did it have to work out this way? Double ugh. One of them had to go to Laken's. And it was looking like she was the one.

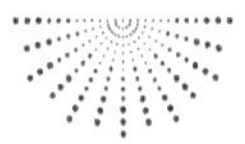

If I don't care about getting to know him better, why am I wasting all this time on my clothes, hair, and makeup?

She parked her car in the parking garage below the apartments and got out, locking the car with a quick chirp.

Good question, and one she wasn't going to answer.

Nope, not going there.

"Hey."

She jumped. "Jesus."

Isaac.

"I didn't mean to scare you."

"You didn't." She released her grip on her bag, realizing she's been clenching it white-knuckled tight. "Much."

"Want an escort?"

She looked around. "Where's your car?"

"Didn't bring it."

Cade cocked her head, eyeing him suspiciously. "Then why are you down here?"

"You're late. Laken was worried. Told her I'd make sure you made it up safely."

Cade couldn't help the laughter that bubbled in her chest and exited her mouth. "She thought a shifter would need help?" She kept her voice low. She lengthened her strides to keep up with his long legs.

"Under certain circumstances, everyone needs help." He pressed the elevator button.

She couldn't argue that, and she didn't know what else to say that would be safe territory. She didn't want to hear about his job, or how close they were to closing the cat burglar case, so she rode in silence, purse clutched in front of her.

"What are you hiding?"

She whirled, her fear outweighing her anger. "What are you talking about?" She barely managed to get the words out without sputtering.

"Hunter's block. You used it last night, and you're using it now. The only time our kind ever use that is when we're hiding something. So what is it?"

A million things flew through her mind—none of them viable. The top of the list was to tell him she was pregnant and trying to hide the scent so her sisters wouldn't know. Cade didn't want to tell him that. Something like that would make him think she had someone else. And that was the last thing she wanted him to think.

"I have my reasons." That was the only thing she could come up with.

His eyes narrowed. Blue diamantine shards studied her.

She squirmed, shifting from one foot to the other. Then anger seized her. Who the hell did he think he was? He had no right to question her.

"Why don't you mind your own business, Officer?"

A slight reaction, the tiniest flinch, told her she'd struck a chord.

"You're right. I'm sorry. It's not my business. Hard to put the shield away, you know?"

She nodded, still suffused with anger. Cade studied the elevator's control panel to keep from looking at him. She hadn't meant to be so abrupt. If he weren't currently working on solving a series of crimes that would put her in prison, she'd be fine with questions.

He's Ky's brother.

For her sister's sake, she should keep the peace.

And it doesn't hurt that I find him sexy.

She counted to three to rein in her temper, then forced a smile to her face and turned his way.

Isaac had been caught off-guard by the ferocity of

her response to his question. Then he chastised himself for not ever allowing the cop in him to rest.

When she turned to him with a smile on her face, he knew instantly it wasn't genuine. And even though she was using hunter's block and he couldn't scent her attraction, he could tell she felt a pull. It showed in the way her eyes dilated and her nostrils flared.

"What do *you* do?" he asked.

An expression flickered across her face, so brief and fleeting he hadn't a clue what it was, then just as quickly, she hid her emotions behind a smile, this time a real one.

"I teach."

He fought the urge to cock his head. To question her more.

I'm a fool. It's not questioning if I just ask her stuff normal people talk about.

"What grade?"

She raised a brow.

"Hey." He raised his hands as if showing a white flag. *And it does feel like I'm surrendering.* "I'm just asking like a guy… you know… not like a cop."

"Kindergarten. But it's winter break now, you know. Christmas and all that."

"Have you done your Christmas shopping yet? That's a safe question, right?"

A laugh escaped her, genuine and captivating. He could watch this fascinating woman for days on end.

"Yes, it's a safe question. Almost done. I'm making a quick run tomorrow for a couple more things. Now that Ky's a part of the family and all that."

The elevator dinged and the doors whooshed open, allowing them a view of the hallway that led to each apartment. Wreaths garnished each door, and pine garlands streamed across the walls. They stepped out of the elevator into the alcove, then turned left to go to Laken's place.

Isaac came to a standstill abruptly. He put a hand on Cade's arm, halting her. He turned to face her, then pointed above her head.

She turned to look at him as if wondering why he'd stopped her, then she tipped her chin and looked upward.

Her lips parted slightly in surprise.

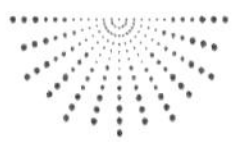

"Oh." Cade's next word was a whisper. "Mistle—"

His mouth cut off the rest of what she was going to say. His tongue didn't seek permission, it invaded with a mission: claim and conquer.

Cade didn't have the time to be surprised by the kiss. Desire burst through her subconscious urge to construct a wall that would keep him out. Her heart pounded so hard she was afraid his shifter hearing would pick it up.

His tongue's insistent exploration of her mouth was intoxicating, and his scent, overwhelming with desire, lit a fire in her that threatened to implode. It had been too long since she'd kissed a man, and she'd never kissed a man like this, a man who clicked with her in every way. His bear reached out to her panther, transcending space and the laws of physics.

No!

She couldn't do this. She couldn't let her panther reveal who she was to his bear. Cade pushed her panther back, sealing her away from the polar bear that was prodding at her mind's recesses.

And yet, no matter how much she pushed, no matter how strong her will was, the flames of passion, the aching need inside her, engulfed her in a cascade that felt like swimming up a waterfall.

The heat of his body surrounded her, and his scent, manly and musky with a hint of pine woods, blended with the scent of his desire and filled her lungs. Cade felt like she couldn't breathe even though she knew oxygen was making its way into her lungs.

Isaac's hands ran down her sides, pulling her firmly against his body, leaving a trail of heat in their wake, making her nerve endings crave his touch.

Cade's hands snaked around his neck, touching his short hair, digging her nails into his scalp, and pulling him down with an intense desire to have more of him, more of this.

"Sorry." A voice interrupted them with the brutality of an ice bucket challenge.

A neighbor of her sister's, some stranger she'd never met before, had stepped out of his apartment.

Heat of embarrassment replaced the flush of desire she'd felt on her cheeks. She jerked her head from

Isaac's but his hands kept her firmly in place, unable to pull away from his body.

"Merry Christmas," Isaac said to the neighbor, who'd turned away and was heading down the hallway, a bottle of wine and two glasses in hand.

"Same to you," the man looked back to say.

"Let me go," Cade hissed.

"We're not done." Blue eyes twinkled with mischief and desire. At the same time, a deep amber glow shone in the depths of his eyes. "You're not going anywhere, now that I have you."

Half of Cade wanted to shove against his chest and hurt him and the other half of her wanted him to pick her up and carry her to the nearest bed, table, wall— you name it, she wanted to experience it with this man. She felt what he wanted to show her, even though he wasn't doing anything deliberate to make it happen. His hardness pressed against her belly, evidence of a desire that made hers stronger.

He two-stepped her backward, without music, pushing her back and back. Unable to do anything but follow, because she didn't want this to end, Cade let him lead her step after step until the unyielding wall was against her back and his huge, muscular body was pressed fully flush against hers, melding her into him.

Cade melted. She'd read about this, heard about this, but—*Ohdeargod*—she'd never thought this could happen to her. No, she wasn't some wilting, yielding, delicate flower…

And yet, this man pressing her against the wall made images fly through her head that were strictly X-rated. Heaven help her, she wanted him. Her panther roared in agreement in the depths of Cade's mind, demanding to be brought further out of her subconscious, fighting her exile.

She bit her lips. Angels in heaven, was he going to kiss her, or was he going to make her suffer?

And with that thought, she could have smacked herself.

When did I become THAT woman?

He raised a hand, slowly gliding it up, starting at her fingertips, trailing it her palm, then the inside of her wrist. He traced tiny circles on the delicate translucent skin there, making goose bumps everywhere else on her body. Shivers raced up her spine while desire pooled between her legs.

He lowered his head and brushed his lips against hers.

"Stop fighting it." His breath was warm.

She breathed it in, taking that part of him inside her deeply, letting it touch her soul. Her eyes closed while she relished the upheaval of unfamiliar emotions.

And then suddenly—

—nothing

—cold

—emptiness.

He'd pulled away and propped his hands on the wall, his arms forming a prison that she'd eagerly and willingly be trapped in.

"The next move will be up to you."

Cade opened her mouth to speak. Okay, not to speak. More like to scream. She was tempted to yell at him, to tell him how little she appreciated the emotional and sensory rollercoaster he'd just taken her on.

Except, by damn, she couldn't. If she gave in, there'd be a hell of a lot more with him. On one hand, she wanted to kill him, but on the other, she wanted to lead him to a private place and—

—And then a door opened and her sister peeked out.

"There you are. I thought you'd gotten lost." Laken gave them a curious look.

Isaac dropped his arms slowly, casually, as if what they'd been doing was completely natural.

Cade swallowed so hard her ears felt like they popped. Luckily, before she could think what to say, Laken had already turned to go back into her apartment.

"You." Cade glared at Isaac.

Then that man did the most infuriating thing.

He laughed.

Her conflicted emotions warred over a response.

Then he walked away; before she could speak, following her sister Laken into her apartment.

What the hell just happened?

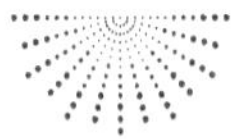

Isaac could barely walk with the erection he had. He tried to think of anything he could to make it vanish before he walked into Laken's place. He followed Laken slowly, so he wouldn't look at the furious Cade. Even when she seethed, she was beautiful. Maybe even more beautiful because that lent perspective as to what her face would look like in the heat of passion.

He fought the unexpected sense of loss at not having her in his arms. If she were his mate, he'd have taken her before they came over here—twice, and then again after they went home. Instead, he was left with the hollow feeling she wasn't completely onboard with their attraction, as if she were fighting it and him at the same time.

She wanted him as fiercely as he wanted her. He

knew this without scenting her emotions. No amount of hunter's block could hide the deliciously female scent that rose from between her legs. If the way she smelled was any indicator, she would taste delicious. His bear roared in agreement.

"Where've you been?" Ky asked him as he walked in the door.

Laken gave Ky *the look.*

Ky clamped his lips into a flat line.

Isaac wasn't about to dig a deeper hole for himself with Cadence. He shrugged. "Need any help?"

"Nah. We're good."

"Sure," Laken disagreed. "Would you mind slicing tomatoes while I blend the soup? Creamy tomato with fresh basil work for you?"

Isaac's stomach grumbled.

"I guess that's a yes." Laken laughed.

The door closed behind him. He didn't need to turn and look. He could feel Cade's presence as if connected to her by electrodes.

"Hey, Ky." Cade hugged her brother-in-law, then her sister. "What can I do?"

"Set the table, if you don't mind." Laken showed Cade where everything was.

She leaned across the table, placing the plates just so, adjusting the knives and forks, giving the mundane task of table-setting more attention and care than it needed. Her hands touched the silverware gently, capturing his imagination.

She'd taken her coat off and was garbed in a pair of black pants that made her hips flare to a delicious apple-shaped ass. Isaac couldn't turn his eyes away. Her hair had slipped out of the ponytail high on her head, and dark tendrils lay against her light olive skin in a canvas of contrast.

Her top was fitted, molding to her breasts in a way he wished his fingers could. The toffee-colored fabric hugged her waist as it tapered, then flared back out again where it lay on her hips.

I'm in trouble.

Yes, he sure was. He'd never felt this for a woman. He had no clue it could be so all-consuming.

"What do you say, Isaac?"

He dropped his eyes to the tomatoes he sure as hell wasn't slicing. "What's that?"

"How about a beer on the balcony when you're done with those? The grill's probably ready for the salmon."

"Sounds good."

Ky placed a beer next to the cutting board. "Incentive."

Isaac made short work of knocking the tomatoes out and avoiding looking at Cade, though her very presence in the room was impossible to ignore when she was so engrained in every cell in his body.

He hustled out to the balcony, inhaling the mesquite wood Ky had added to the fire.

"You've got it bad," Ky said. "Reminds me how it was with Laken. Couldn't think of anything but her."

"Now she's yours."

"One day, Cade will be yours." Ky tapped his longneck against Isaac's and nodded his *cheers.*

"I don't think so. They're very different women. And I can tell you that Cadence barely likes me."

"That's not how I see it." Ky put the water-soaked cedar plank on the grill. "You'd be surprised by Laken. She's a lot more like Cade than you think. They're passionate women; they both live for their causes. Find out what Cade's cause is, and join her."

Isaac took a draw from the longneck. Even though alcohol didn't affect shifters, that didn't stop him from enjoying the flavor. "She teaches kindergarten. What kind of cause could she have?" *Collecting colored pencils?* But he didn't voice his thought. He knew it was based on frustration.

Isaac knew she was deep. He got that she was passionate, but damn it, how was he supposed to penetrate those fucking defenses of hers?

I'm so screwed.

"I have to make it an early night," Isaac told Ky.

Ky looked up from the grill. "What's up?"

"We may have a chance to catch that cat burglar. There's talk about a large amount of cash being around after an auction." Isaac kept a bead on Cadence leaning against the counter talking to Laken, her face animated and excited.

"Damn. Sounds interesting."

"Why don't you come along? I'm going solo and your special ops training might come in handy. It's not department-approved. One of the perks of leading a Special Task Force—I get a lot of latitude, as long as I get results."

"Hell, yeah. I'll go! Hang on." Ky opened the sliding glass door and peeked in. "Hey, mind if I go out on a case with Isaac tonight?"

Laken gave him a nod, then walked over, leaving Cadence alone. "What time?"

Ky looked at Isaac for an answer.

"Eleven."

"Is this…"

"Police business." Isaac left it at that.

CADE WATCHED ISAAC. His hands were in his pockets and he leaned forward, the fabric straining against the muscles of his back. His ass was perfect, the kind she'd seen on calendars when she was in college. The kind that made it onto those birthday cards in the *special* area of the card section.

"What was that about?" she asked Laken. Because if

it involved Isaac, she wanted to know—for more reasons than one.

Cade kept her gaze glued on Isaac. He turned her way, locking eyes with her, as if he knew she'd been watching him and was letting her know he knew. Excitement flowed throughout her body at the directness of his gaze.

"Guess it's not going to be a late night. Isaac has to go to work, and Ky's going with him."

A shiver of the totally horrible kind started at the base of her spine and traveled the length of her back. "What kind of work?"

"Police business. That's all Isaac said, but if I had to make a guess, I'd say it was that cat burglar case that's been plaguing him."

Her earlier excitement was replaced with dread. "Why does it bother him so much?" When Laken gave her a look, Cade tried to dig herself out. "I mean… I get that he's a cop and that's his job and all, but the whole 'plaguing' thing, isn't that carrying it too far?"

"Pretty sure the fact he suspects it's one of our kind is what gets to him."

Why can't he leave well enough alone?

And tonight of all nights, a night she planned to do a job. She knew exactly where a nice amount of cash would be located. Two more good jobs like the one she planned tonight and she'd be done. She'd have reached her goal.

Then I'll put the cat burglar gig away for good.

She had to; it was killing her ability to look the man she was attracted to in the eye, the man her panther insisted was her fated mate.

Just a couple more times to fully fund a home for children in abusive situations. Just a couple more jobs would provide for the place that could assist little ones. No child should have to deal with the things she'd seen little Ignacio go through before he was killed.

Pinpricks tormented her eyelids, threatening to yield to a gush of tears. She swallowed them back.

"I can't stay late tonight either."

Laken gave her a weird look. "Last month you were frustrated that you don't get to see me enough, and now I'm in town and you can't stay late."

"I'm sorry." Cade wrapped her arms around her sister and hugged her.

Would Laken understand if she told her about Ignacio? And why she was leaving early? And what she did?

If she tried, then Laken would want to know how Cade had come to be what she was, how she'd become a thief.

No, she wasn't ready to share her life with her sister.

CHAPTER SEVEN

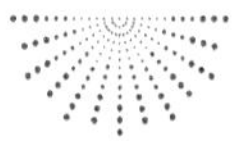

Isaac was aware of Cade's presence during dinner like one is aware they're in a tornado. He couldn't push the influence of her from his mind or his body. And his bear sure as hell wouldn't let Isaac push the effect away.

The bastard.

Isaac and his bear hadn't had an easy time of it. Their relationship had been strained when he was growing up. They always seemed to be at odds, and more often than not, Isaac pushed his bear aside and silenced him.

His brother Ky had an easier time with his bear. They'd always been close; they'd been best friends and inseparable, always in each other's heads. Ky's bear guided him throughout life. Which wasn't to say everything was easy for Ky; Isaac knew it wasn't. His time in the Middle East had taken its toll on Ky.

Isaac didn't care much for his bear until he'd turned twenty. Even then, it was a grudgingly given compromise that characterized their relationship.

Probably both of us are too damned hardheaded, Isaac mused.

Next to him, Cade took a bite, her arm brushing against his. Electric currents raced through his veins, leaving him charged. He took a bite of the salmon, knowing it tasted good, but he couldn't tell for his senses were centered on her.

His bear was practically purring in his mind, content to be near her.

What the fuck? Bears don't purr.

"Aunt Miriam's expecting us at eleven on Christmas day," Laken was saying.

Isaac forced himself to pay attention, noting that Laken called her Aunt Miriam, glad that she'd fit into the Romanoff clan as easily as she had. They weren't always an easy bunch to get along with, he was the first to admit. Not with their characteristic bullheadedness. His last two girlfriends could bear witness to that. Of course, Aunt Miriam argued, they had never deserved him.

She spent so much time making Isaac, Ky, and Jonah feel like her own kids, taking the three rambunctious boys on after their parents had gone.

"I'll be there," Isaac said. He turned toward Cadence. "You're going, right?"

Cade wouldn't look at him. She didn't answer right away.

"Of course, she is." Laken shot him a glance, as if that was a stupid question. "Are you done with your Christmas shopping?" she asked him.

"It looks like I'm not. I don't have anything for Cadence or Carina."

"You don't need to worry about me. I have everything I need," Cade responded.

"Don't be such a Scrooge." Laken harrumphed and gave her a dirty look. "You know what you should do? Go Christmas shopping together tomorrow. That way, you can help Isaac pick up something for Carina, too. And you can tell him what you want, since you have everything you need."

THE LOOK in Laken's eyes screamed manipulation and matchmaking.

I'm going to kill my sister.

Cade worked a tight smile to her lips. "Sure." She knew she probably sounded petulant.

He only wants to put me in jail for a very long time. Why don't I hang out with him and give him the evidence to do so?

Another dirty look from Laken. Cade couldn't blame her sister, but Laken just didn't get it.

The rest of the dinner was a hushed affair for Cade. Except that although she was silent, her panther wasn't, turning tight circles filled with frustration in Cade's mind. Snarling every so often, and roaring once or twice.

Her panther wasn't the only thing that distracted Cade. Every damned time she raised her fork to take a bite, her arm nudged Isaac's.

Why couldn't we flip spots? Having a left-handed and a right-handed person in this arrangement led to nothing but murmured apologies.

Every brush against each other, no matter how incidental, created a blizzard of sensations in Cade. Shivers left goose bump trails on her spine, while neutrons, protons, and electrons ran amok, bouncing around her body, sending signals she wished she could put a damper on.

No such luck. There was no controlling the vibrations that ran rampant.

When the night was over, and the cleanup was done, she breathed a sigh of relief as Isaac and Ky left for their "police business."

Fifteen minutes after the men had said their goodbyes, Cade hugged her sister and told her she'd see her tomorrow, then headed down to the parking garage.

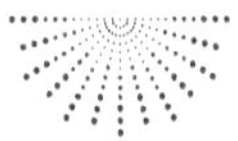

Isaac and Ky were hidden on the rooftop they'd set up as a surveillance post.

Isaac was confident the thief would jump from one of the two adjacent buildings, taking the leap to the building he'd set up surveillance from. They'd changed into black, foregoing any bulletproofing because that would kill some of their running speed if there was a foot chase.

Plus, Isaac felt confident this criminal did not resort to violence. He didn't want to admire the thief, but he did feel a grudging sense of respect. The criminal was clean and neat, only robbed the rich, and never hurt anyone.

What the hell is wrong with me? He's a damned criminal. I don't feel respect for perps.

They'd been here almost two hours. The hour that the thief usually hit was coming up.

Isaac scratched his unshaved scruff. He felt Ky's eyes on him. "Go ahead, say what's on your mind."

"We've been here for a couple of hours. You sure he'll show?"

"I set bait out, planted the right info with the right people. The thing I don't get is, no one will flip on him. Not one single person will admit to knowing him. Why not?"

Ky's expression didn't sit well with Isaac.

"Say what you're thinking."

"I'm wondering if you're a little…" Ky let a heavy breath out, as if he was carrying a huge burden. "Obsessed, maybe. If not, then tell me why you don't have a team out here. Or backup."

"I don't have to. I told you that."

"Yeah, I know, but common sense would dictate you'd have some. Unless you don't want them to know how much effort you're plugging into this."

Isaac shook his head—except he wasn't just shaking it at Ky. He was shaking it at his bear too, who wouldn't shut the hell up about Cade.

"If you really need to talk, let's shift and sync."

Isaac shifted into his bear so Ky would too. After Ky shifted, he sent a signal that bumped into Isaac's mind, trying to establish a link. They couldn't communicate unless both shifted creatures enabled the link.

Isaac looked around carefully and inhaled deeply to be sure there were no onlookers. The last thing he needed was some human to witness two large polar bears on a rooftop in New York City. That would get ugly.

Happy now? Ky asked him silently.

I don't want this jeopardized. I'd like to close this case. If I do, then I'm a shoe-in for a spot with InterForce. I'd like to be in a paranormal unit there. Like you were, in Sigma Eps.

Ky had served in Sigma Eps, a military unit composed of paranormal individuals. Humans didn't know the unit wasn't simply human. That wasn't discussed, but within the Sigma Eps, nearly impossible missions were brought to a successful end.

Have you talked to Jonah? He'd help you.

Their brother Jonah was in Unit 13, the paranormal unit in InterForce. In this case too, the humans in InterForce had no idea the unit was paranormal.

I didn't want to make it on his coattails. I want to make it based on my achievements.

For fuck's sake, Isaac. You're plenty decorated and you've got a killer resume. You wouldn't be getting it because of Jonah.

I'd rather do it my way.

Suit yourself. So what are you going to do about Cade?

What do you want me to do? Hit her on the head with a club? Drag her by the hair to the nearest cave and take her?

Except for the hitting part, what's wrong with the rest of it? Ky laughed, the sound reverberating in Isaac's head.

As soon as Ky stopped laughing, Isaac gave him his opinion. *I don't think that will work for her.*

A sound caught Isaac's attention. The tiniest of clicks. *Did you hear that?*

Ky glanced around. *No.*

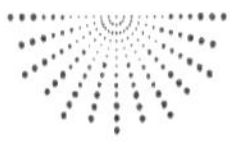

Another day at work. A dozen and a half bundles of energy had pushed her to near exhaustion.

Cade glanced at the phone. She was in the alley behind the targeted home.

Almost two o'clock. Almost go time.

Clothing: All black.

Hunter's block: In effect.

Backpack with lock picking kit: packed.

Change of clothing: Check.

She'd really misspent her youth; she knew that. After their parents had died, Laken, Cadence, and Carina had been split up. No relative volunteered to take all three girls, so they'd gone to different relatives' homes, not reuniting until they'd grown.

Laken had gone to one set of grandparents, Carina to the other set.

Cadence was left with her father's younger brother, who had found her to be an adorable decoy while he plied and plowed his way through rich widows and bored housewives. After a few years, Cade wasn't the cute little decoy anymore.

It was time for Uncle Ramon to include her in a completely different enterprise. She had a new place in her uncle's plans.

Accessory.

She learned the ins and outs of lock picking, alarm disengagement, scaling buildings, and safe cracking. It didn't hurt that she, like her uncle, was a black panther shifter. Scaling buildings was easy to manage when a single leap could take her to the second-story balcony. It also didn't hurt that she could jump building to building, so even if she was pursued, it was a matter of a leap humans couldn't handle that could put her out of reach of the cops.

And then one day, Uncle Ramon vanished. Poof. Gone. Sixteen-year-old Cade was left to fend for herself. And fend for herself she did.

She didn't put the knowledge her uncle had given her to use. He'd stashed plenty of money, artifacts, and jewelry in a storage unit. She knew his contacts and had no problem fencing items to live. So she finished high school, forging his signature when a guardian's signature was required.

She kept contact with her sisters, but they'd been raised in other areas and had "normal" family lives, so she didn't let them know her situation. They'd email and call, and she'd pretend everything was as it should be.

Then came college. She had no clue what she wanted to do until she spent a summer working as a camp counselor at the Y. Teaching. That was what she wanted.

A few years later, she was doing just that: teaching kindergarten in one of the more underserved, financially deprived areas in the city.

She thought she loved the job until she saw little Ignacio and his daily bruises. She looked into it, tried to find his home. He was classified as homeless, with no address in the system. *A temporary situation,* the school told her, a situation that would be rectified when the boy and his mother were reunited with his father. But still she worried, and she wanted to follow him, to use her panther scenting to track him at night, but...

Time wasn't on her side.

One day, Ignacio quit coming to school.

Two days later, she found out he was being buried that Saturday. She went to the funeral. His mother's silent tears didn't move Cade any more than his mother had been moved to protect Ignacio when he needed her. The boy's stepfather was standing by her side, his face stoic. Cade didn't need anyone to tell her he was the cause of Ignacio's death.

The father appeared at the funeral too. A long distance truck driver, he'd been out of town. Word had it he was trying to find a way to gain custody of his son, and the reasons he didn't were plentiful and understandable: his job, no one at home to watch the child, no stable home environment…

The reasons weren't as heartbreaking as the final result.

When the father appeared at the gravesite, he lunged for the stepfather, screaming accusations of abuse. The stepfather's friends stepped up, and the father was unconscious and being kicked repeatedly before anyone could react.

Cade left the cemetery that afternoon with two goals. The first was immediate. She took care of that matter within a few days, after Ignacio's father had left town on his next long-distance haul. She wanted him long gone, with a solid alibi.

The stepfather's disappearance remained a mystery.

The second goal was taking longer, much longer, but the special home she wanted to fund, Ignacio's Place, was to be more than a dream soon. She was so close to meeting the goal, she could taste it.

Slow down, she cautioned herself, because she knew if she rushed, she'd leave herself open to errors. Like

Uncle Ramon had taught her, she'd be careful and methodical.

She glanced at the burner phone. Straight up two o'clock. She took a deep breath, powered down the phone.

Cade made her way across the building's roof until she found the perfect hiding place for her phone. She set her it in a crack between two cinderblocks next to a large condensing unit.

Though the phone was powered down, she still didn't want to risk it falling into the wrong hands. Somehow, they'd figure out it was hers, and there would be no talking her way out of anything if her phone was found at the crime scene.

She kept the backpack light, because although her clothes shifted with her, the backpack never did. After she shifted, she carried the backpack in her powerful panther jaws. God knew she'd tried to figure out how to get the backpack to shift when she did her. No luck.

If I could figure out the mechanics of shifting while carrying stuff, I'd have a leg up on this.

She slipped out of the stairwell and onto the roof of the building that was next to her targeted building. She'd shift into her panther skin and leap across, then she'd leap from balcony to balcony for fourteen stories.

If she was lucky, the balcony door would be open. *Why would they feel the need to lock it, forty-four flights up?* If she wasn't that lucky, she'd pick the lock and disarm the alarm. She knew the model they used, thanks to a handy, nicely compensated hacker who'd cracked into the databases of several alarm companies.

Thanks to the same guy, she also knew where the control panel had been placed. Too bad the passwords weren't kept online. That would save her a few seconds, though she wasn't particularly worried about time, since the homeowners were said to be wintering in Florida.

A few paces from the rooftop's edge, she slipped behind another unit, took off her backpack, and shifted into her panther.

Ready? she asked her panther. The feline chuffed, eager to get started.

She picked up the backpack between sharp canines, made sure her grip was tight, then crept toward the very edge of the roof, the city's lights twinkling in the background.

She lowered her powerful body, backing to get short running distance, muscles bunching in preparation. She catapulted herself forward, not looking down at what would be certain death.

That leap sent Cade safely onto the other building with distance to spare. She turned back to look at the ledge, her panther eyes glittering dangerously in the dimness.

She padded away from the edge of the building toward a condensing unit, slipped behind it and shifted back into her human form with an almost imperceptible tearing and crunching sound as bones, tendons, and flesh reformed. Then she adjusted her clothing and secured her black mask.

She snatched up the backpack before it could land on the ground and make any noise. That feat and the act of controlling the amount of noise she made when she shifted were courtesy of Uncle Ramon.

He'd made her practice and practice, over and over again, thousands of times, until he was satisfied she could perform the tasks to his satisfaction. Those were only two of the many skills Uncle Ramon drilled into her so she could perform her jobs with ease, confidence, and most importantly, success.

Slipping the backpack over her shoulders, she tightened the strap. She'd take the service stairs down eight flights, then enter an apartment she knew was empty. There, she'd shift again and make her way along the ledge that would take her around the building to the apartment that held the bounty.

Nothing to it.

She needed to not think that way. Being overconfident could be disastrous. Uncle Ramon had warned her of that repeatedly.

Eight flights of stairs and one hallway later, she made a right turn and was in front of the vacant apartment. She slipped her lockpicking kit out of the backpack, then, with a few low ticks of the tumblers as she worked on them, the door unlocked. Glancing around, she verified there were no witnesses and opened the door.

She entered and closed the door behind her with a soft click. Her shifter vision allowed her to see the empty room, find and unlatch the window nearest to the narrow ledge.

Stealthily, she left the vacant apartment behind and made her way along the ledge. Her surefooted panther had no problem retaining her balance as she put paw in front of paw. Several feet later, she was at the first balcony.

She leapt over the railing, then back onto the ledge. Ledge to balcony to ledge, she eased into the routine.

Two corners to turn, then the third balcony she came to would be the one. Less than twenty minutes later she'd leapt onto the balcony and shifted into her human form. And even though she felt confident the luxury apartment would be empty, old habits died hard and she caught the backpack before it touched the tiled balcony floor.

Lockpick set out, she was inside within seconds and zipping toward the room that had the control panel. Once the brass plate that hid the panel was open, she disengaged the blinking alarm.

Then and only then did Cade pause to take a breath, after which, she let it out in a flood of relief. It never failed: no matter how many times she'd done this, each time was a rush, each time was a failure waiting to happen. The hairs on the back of her neck stood up, like they always did.

She paused, letting her sensitive shifter hearing listen for heartbeats and pulses.

Nothing.

The area was clear.

Cade hustled to the bedroom and spotted the large TV that hid the safe. She grabbed the remote and flipped the button which brought the TV forward and revealed a safe in the area behind the TV.

These manufacturers. They'd have been better off not putting everything online where it could be accessed so easily by a good hacker. Paper copies in files would have served them better in cases like this.

First she'd need to determine the contact points on the lock.

Thank goodness for shifter hearing.

She peeled the mask off, because a barrier over her ears wouldn't help, then listened for the click to determine which numbers on the dial face corresponded to the contact area left and right of the notch that allowed the lever to pass through when it was spun.

Now for the parking position. She paid attention to the number of clicks each time the dial passed the parking position opposite the contact area.

She zipped through the process not realizing how quickly she did it, how professionally and effortlessly, until she'd completed the last step and had all the numbers in the combination. Now it was a matter of testing out variations of those numbers until she got the right one.

One pull on the lever on the third combination, and ta-da! She was in.

Cade shoved cash and jewelry into her bag. Just a few seconds more, and she'd re-arm the alarm and slip out, leaving the same way she came in.

An image entered her mind that she wished hadn't. Isaac's face.

Really? He's going to make me feel guilty?

She pushed the image away and remembered little Ignacio's face. Not the way he'd looked in the open casket, but the way he'd looked when he'd drawn a picture of Cade with a black panther behind her. Of course the little boy hadn't known the significance of that picture, but he'd never know how close it struck the heart of Cade and her panther.

She opened the door, stepped onto the balcony and pulled her mask on. Setting the heavier backpack on the floor, she shifted into her panther and seized the bag between her teeth. Almost done. Now came the trek along the ledges and balconies back to the empty apartment, then a few flights up to the rooftop, a leap across, changing her clothing, and home.

She could taste freedom.

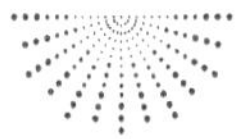

CHAPTER TEN

In bear form, the two men waited patiently. A shadow appeared on the wall cattycorner from Isaac and Ky.

Isaac heard the tiniest of taps again. He synced his brother. *You heard that. Tell me you didn't.*

I did.

A silhouette shaped like a large feline. A slight tap.

Holy shit. Look!

The silhouette shifted into—

A woman. Goddammit. That's a woman.

There was no mistaking the curvy form clad all in black. It was all woman. What kind of cat had it been? He'd only seen the silhouette. Not a tiger, he didn't think. Damn, it was so quick and subtle, he hadn't caught what kind of cat she was.

I take it the task force had no idea the cat burglar could be female?

Not a clue. Let's shift. I need to apprehend this criminal.

He shifted and a second behind him, Ky shifted as well, both of them emitting the slight creaks and crunches associated with shifting.

The woman in black who was striding across the rooftop froze. She'd heard them shift. She glanced around, her movements nervous and quick.

"Stop. NYPD." Isaac strode out of the shadows.

A gasp came out of her mouth and she took off at a run, her backpack in hand. She rounded a corner a few yards ahead of him. By the time he'd turned the corner, Ky on his heels, the woman was gone and all he saw was the cat's figure in the shadows of the building across the alley. With a flick of her tail, the feline was gone.

Isaac grabbed the ledge, looking over the abyss of concrete below. He kept his eyes glued to the spot he'd last seen the feline.

"Now what?" Ky asked. "Give chase?"

Isaac grunted. "We're fucking bears. We don't leap. We power our way through obstacles."

"This isn't a situation we can power ourselves through. Too bad you don't have a team, or backup, or anything."

Isaac gave Ky a look. He didn't need to be reminded

of that. "We need a cat shifter to make the leap and give chase. Would Laken help?"

Ky looked at him as if he'd lost it. "She's got three legs. I'm not going to ask her to do that. What if she didn't make the leap across? What are you thinking? You would endanger Laken's life?"

Guilt flushed through Isaac. *I'm a dick for suggesting that.*

"No. Sorry. I wasn't thinking."

"You know…" Ky scratched his head, his eyes also focused on the building on the other side. "We could use a tranq. I know how to get my hands on some."

"Not a bad idea." Isaac thought about it. It might be frowned upon, as shifters didn't like to hear about other shifters being tranqed. But he'd take that risk.

"Except there's something we didn't think of…" Ky said. "…she's not going to let us see her again."

"Unless I set up irresistible bait."

"Sounds like you have a plan."

"I do."

"You don't think she'll be too spooked, after tonight?"

"Nah. I'll just have to make sure it's worth her time."

*S*HIT.

Shit. Shit.

Cade recognized his voice. She knew it was Isaac.

What the hell is he doing on the rooftop?

She ran around the corner, shifted quickly, grabbed the backpack and ran toward the edge of the building, spanning the distance and landing with an impact that was off somehow. She lay on the concrete for all of a second while the burn ate at her arm. But no, she'd been sure the leap wasn't a big deal.

She found out just how much her jump had been off when she shifted and tried to pick up her backpack with her left hand.

Fuck.

Fuck. Fuck.

Her wrist. It was so screwed. She'd hit the concrete with far too much force and at the wrong angle. It didn't help that she'd tried to look back mid-leap and had landed awkwardly. Now, her left hand hung loosely at her side, seeping blood, a sliver of white showing through.

Bone. Just great. Just fucking great.

Her only option now was to shift and heal. In their animal form, shifters could heal most serious injuries. They'd go into a state similar to hibernation while their bodies repaired themselves.

She was happy she had an arm that could heal. Laken had never stood a chance. Her sister's entire leg had been blown off in the Middle East. Even after she'd shifted, when she had come to, there was still no leg.

At least I'll have an arm when it's all said and done.

She grabbed a bandana from the backpack and wrapped it around her arm to stop the blood from leaking everywhere, and took off for the stairs that led to the ground floor. She'd have to run, because she was sure Isaac and Ky would be following her.

What the shit.

Isaac was there. How the hell had he known where she'd be?

She pushed the thought aside. She needed to get home. Immediately. She surged forward, taking the steps two at a time, the backpack slung over her right shoulder.

When she reached the ground floor, she looked around to be sure an ambush wasn't waiting for her.

So far so good.

She slipped out the back door of the apartment building and onto the empty street. Hugging walls, she shot down the block toward her parked car. Every step wrenched at the broken bone in her wrist.

Finally, she was home. She locked the door to her bedroom in case Cari came in, then dropped the backpack on the floor, kicked it under the bed, and shifted into her panther.

She limped to the other side of the bed, lay where she'd be out of sight of the door, and sank into oblivion.

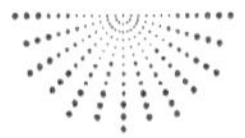

Cade stretched and yawned in her panther form, and noted she could put weight on her front leg. All that bore witness to last night's injuries was a white scar near her wrist.

She shifted into her human skin and stripped her black clothing off.

She grabbed the dirty and bloody clothing and walked to the laundry room in just her bra and panties. She didn't pay attention to the voices she heard in the living room. Probably Cari on the phone while watching TV.

Cade had just put the clothes into the washer and dropped the lid when she turned around and found herself face to face with Isaac.

Isaac!

She bit back the squeal of surprise and shock that threatened to erupt from her throat and jumped back.

He was looking at her with a curious and amused look on his face. Those light blue eyes saw right through her, clear to the very essence of her desire for him. Her throat worked, but she couldn't get a sound out. Sand and sawdust gathered, blocking her words. That wasn't the least of what he did to her. He was so damned gorgeous. That chiseled jaw, those sculpted cheekbones.

Then she realized she was wearing nothing but a bra and panties and her throat decided to function once more.

"Oh, God."

She grabbed for whatever was hanging off the wooden post that ran the length of the washroom and wrapped it around her body.

"What the hell? What are you doing here?"

"Sorry."

He didn't look one damned bit sorry.

Nope, not sorry at all.

He looked hot. And sexy. And so very…

Ugh.

Away with that line of thought. Away with it.

Cari walked in. She looked at Cade. "Oh."

Cade gave her a dirty look, like *you set me up.*

Cari looked down. "I didn't know… I'm sorry."

Haven't you fucked up my life enough?

"Why are you here?" Cade asked Isaac, her tone scalding, and at the same time battling with a primal yearning for him.

"Lunch? Christmas shopping?" he reminded her.

Cade found herself fuming at her sister. *Damn it, Laken, this is all your fault.* "I'm not ready."

"You weren't answering your phone…"

Her phone was off and lying on the nightstand by her bed.

Oh, hell. Then she remembered the burner phone that she'd left on the rooftop. She'd left it there because she never carried anything that could be directly linked to her to the sites. If it were somehow lost or taken—she'd be screwed. It was still on the rooftop on that building. Cade wanted to growl in frustration. This sucked.

"Could I have some privacy?"

How can I back out of this?

"I'll wait for you in the living room." He turned and walked out before Cade could come up with an out.

Cari followed him before Cade could signal to her to stay so she could beg Cari to take her place. With a silent, sullen growl, Cade headed to her room and changed into a pair of jeans and a sweater.

When she got to the living room, Isaac was sprawled on the sofa, head back, eyes closed, breathing softly. His unapproachable, tough guy face had lost its predatory look. His wide chest rose and fell rhythmically.

Cade approached him, moving softly on the rug to keep from waking him. It figured he was tired, since he'd spent his night trying to hunt her down. Stopping directly in front of him, she stared at him, at the broad shoulders that tapered to what she could only guess would be a lovely vee.

Damn. Damn. Damn.

It had been way too long since she'd been with a man, or even thought of being with one. Her eyes and her panther feasted on the sight in front of her.

God, I could crawl on him and straddle...

His eyes flew open, blue diamond lasers with a golden flash in their depths.

She flinched at the intensity of his look. Air caught at the back of her throat, and she struggled to speak. "You fell asleep. Long night?"

"Work. You just woke up, so how about you?"

"None of your business," she snapped. Yeah, she was still angry about last night, about being his prey. "Where's my sister?"

"Said she had an errand."

Bullshit. Cade recognized what Carina and Laken were both doing. Damn them and their matchmaking. But Carina should know better. Carina knew he was trying to capture her.

"Lunch or shopping first?"

Cade was going to tell him they should pass on lunch and knock out the shopping until her stomach growled so loudly, even a human with their inferior hearing would have heard it across the room.

"Lunch it is," he said, and smiled.

That smile. Those lips curving up in a way that made her heart skip a beat…

I am so screwed. So very royally screwed.

Isaac followed her out of her apartment. He couldn't resist checking out her curves. Those hips he wanted to put his hands on…

The ass he'd like to…

Fuck. I'd better quit this before I get into all sorts of trouble.

His bear growled, but not necessarily in agreement.

Isaac didn't want to push his luck by suggesting a romantic venue since she'd snapped at him a few times already.

Someone got up on the wrong side of the bed today.

He wondered what had happened to put the curvy beauty in such a bad mood.

She suggested a place nearby.

A few moments later, he took a ravenous bite of the sandwich he'd ordered at the deli a few blocks from her place. Then he remembered: he hadn't had breakfast.

On the other hand, for someone whose stomach had growled so fiercely earlier, she seemed to be interested in nothing more than picking at her food, shifting the chips around on her plate, and plucking tiny morsels of the sandwich between her fingertips before daintily placing them between her lips.

Okay, no lie, she's turning me on.

He averted his gaze from her mouth because this wasn't working. He couldn't spend lunch turned on.

She picked up her sandwich, brought it close to her mouth. "So, how's your case?" She took a bite.

He looked into her eyes. *Where's this going?* Why the casual conversation now?

"It's a woman."

She gasped. Her sandwich fell to the deli paper, split apart and scattered its fixings. She looked down at the sandwich and tried to reassemble it, a messy endeavor.

"That's a useless cause." The sandwich was beyond repair. "Let me order you another one," he offered.

"Oh, no. I'm not really very hungry."

He studied her face. "You sure?"

She nodded, but her face was so pale that it made him wonder if she was sick.

"Can I trust you?

She coughed. "Sure."

"I need help."

Her eyes grew wide. "From me? What kind of help can a kindergarten teacher offer you? My specialties are corralling little children and trying to organize paperwork during reading time." A forced smile curved her lips.

He laughed, though she didn't seem amused. "No, I think it's safer to say I need your shifter skills more than I do your teacher skills."

CADE FOUGHT to keep her hand from shaking as she raised a chip to her mouth. She put it back down. She'd probably choke on the damned thing.

"My shifter skills?" *Why does my voice sound so squeaky?* Yeah, like she didn't know.

"It seems the cat burglar—"

"Who is a shifter and a woman…" She couldn't help cutting him off. "And you're sure of that?"

"Yeah. Very. I saw her last night. She's definitely a woman. All woman."

Cade wasn't sure she cared for the appreciative gleam in his eyes when he said that. She knew she was the one… but he didn't. "Why didn't you catch her, then?"

"For starters, we didn't have the… Well, it was just me and Ky. I didn't have anyone else there."

"It wasn't an official thing, then?"

"That's one way to put it."

"And she got away with it? Whatever she stole?"

"This time." His jaw clenched. He most definitely wasn't happy with that situation.

"So I don't get where my help would come in handy."

"She's a feline shifter—"

"What kind?"

He gave her a look, as if he was wondering why she kept interrupting him. "I don't know. It was dark, and she was quick."

Thank God. "So what do you need me for?"

"I just thought of it when I came into your place. I can't jump from building to building like she does. Bears don't jump. You can."

"And you want me to risk my life jumping between buildings to catch a common cat burglar that the NYPD can't?" She shook her head. "And you see nothing wrong with asking me that?"

At least he had the decency to look chagrined. "You have a point." He scratched his days-old growth of beard.

Why does he have to be so sexy when he does that?

"There's another option. I could ask my brother if there's anyone in Unit 13 with InterForce who could help out." He didn't look thrilled with the idea.

"But you'd rather not."

"It doesn't fall into their jurisdiction. They might be

able to help, off the books, but I'd rather make the collar myself."

"What harm is this criminal really doing, Isaac? Is she stealing from people who are hungry and poor? How do you know she's not doing something good with the proceeds?"

"It's a crime."

"It's black and white for you, just like that?"

He looked up from his sandwich and stopped his hand mid-air, almost ready to take a bite.

"No exceptions?" she pressed further.

"None I can think of, right off the top of my head."

"You should think harder." She bit her tongue and clamped her lips shut.

He studied her face, his expression somber. "Working with little children has given you an amazingly innocent perspective."

If you only knew. "I always root for the underdog. Let's go." She pushed her chair back with a loud scraping sound. "We have shopping to do."

He held the door open for her as they exited the deli.

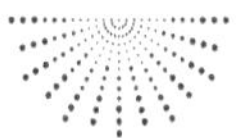

Hours later… had it really been hours? She'd actually enjoyed the normally tortuous task of shopping. She'd had a good time, and it was because of Isaac. They'd laughed, his earlier request forgotten, and they'd shopped for gifts for each other's families. They'd spent hours and hours, and yet, it didn't feel like it.

He put his hand on her arm just after they'd exited the last store.

The beginnings of dusk were making the city darken as he pulled her into an alcove. Tiny snowflakes swirled around them, creating a magical environment where dreams and wishes could come true.

But dreams and wishes don't come true. Cade knew better.

"Cadence."

She loved the way he said her name, not short and choppy like she insisted everyone else say it. On his tongue, it was a caress that flowed through her and then pulled her in for an embrace.

She looked at this man, her enemy, her hunter, and if her panther was right, her fated mate.

Inside, her body was a jumble of nerves. How did he make her feel this way? It wasn't sex. No, not just sex, but all of what she felt for him met in that one place, deep within her, that spanned from the tip of her toes to her brain.

I'm crazy. This is crazy. This can't end well.

He raised a hand, put it behind her neck, and moved it slowly, leaving tiny goose bumps in her flesh that had nothing whatsoever to do with the temperature. Shivers raced down her back. Those translucent blue eyes of his held her captive while his hand traveled until it cupped her cheek with such tenderness, her breath refused to leave her body.

She forced herself to breathe out.

Big mistake, because then she had to breathe in.

And what she breathed in was all Isaac, all male, all sexiness, blended with the scent of woods and peppermint.

Heaven help her. She was falling.

"Cadence."

That word again. Her name, the way he said it, was an aphrodisiac of the greatest proportions.

"There's something about you. There's something here. Tell me you don't feel it."

She hesitated.

Perhaps too long, because before she could formulate a response, he lowered his head, tilting it just so, and swiped his tongue over her lips.

At first she thought he'd be gentle, as if asking permission, but that wasn't Isaac's way, it seemed. He pressed forward, pushing her against the wall, his mouth staking his claim on her, his tongue acting out his desire. He pressed against her, trapping her. His tongue did the eternal dance with hers, a tango that built a fire within her. The kiss seemed to last forever as his other hand drifted to her waist and pulled her against the length of him.

Oxygen was making its way to her lungs, she was sure, because she hadn't passed out, but at the same time she felt breathless. She couldn't concentrate on anything but the man in front of her.

He pulled back, his gaze on fire. Her lips were cold in the absence of his.

"I'd like to take you to dinner."

Dinner?

She couldn't even fathom the idea of dinner. She took a deep breath to clear her thinking.

No. She had to retrieve her phone. She needed to…

She didn't know what she needed.

Yes, she did. She most certainly did.

She needed to run away from him as fast as she could before he trapped her in…

Heaven.

One more deep breath, more head clearing—or at least a valiant effort to do so.

"I can't tonight. I have something to do."

He nodded slowly, as if he didn't buy that.

"About your request, though…" she continued.

"Request?"

"To help you. With catching your cat burglar. I'll do it."

I'm crazy.

She wanted to shake herself. What was she thinking? "Just give me a few days to get some things wrapped up."

Like maybe a final job so that I can officially retire from my life of crime and get Ignacio's Place funded.

"You're sure about dinner?" His lips brushed hers.

No. I need to get my phone. And get last night's bounty to Ben.

Ben, her liaison.

Who am I kidding? He's a fence. Used to be Uncle Ramon's fence.

"I can't." She left it at that.

Moments later, she'd left him on the corner.

THE STRUGGLE between wanting Isaac and trying to avoid being arrested by him was tearing Cade up.

Getting the burner phone back was no big deal. There wasn't anyone watching the building next to the one she'd robbed.

Cade powered it on while she strode toward her apartment.

She had a text.

Ben: Want another lead?

She called him. "The last lead almost got me arrested."

"This isn't from the same guy. And it's a big one."

"Keep talking." *Is this the answer to my prayers? The last job?*

"*Hey*, I can only tell you what I know. I can't tell you what the cops know or plan. Do you want it or not?"

I should wait. I should let more time go by.

Yeah, but if I take this one and wrap it up, I can be done with it.

And she could enjoy the holiday season. And maybe enjoy time with Isaac, because she wouldn't be his target anymore.

Those two thoughts, holiday season and Isaac, merged with one word: mistletoe.

Damn him. Yeah, she should get this over with, do the last job, get Ignacio's Place started, and then…

She sighed. "Go on, let's have it."

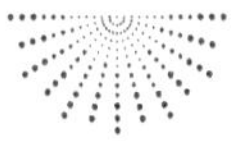

Isaac walked toward his desk. The station was a hub of noise and activity. He tuned it out, setting his coffee down, booting up his computer. Paperwork. The bane of his existence.

Though the banc would have been a cat burglar, his bear reminded him.

He shoved the smartass back.

"Mister?"

He barely registered the tiny voice calling out. In fact, safe to say he tuned it out.

A tug on his sleeve made that hard to do. He turned his attention toward a seven-year-old with a grimy face and grimier nails.

"What's up?"

Bright eyes in a curious face regarded him with that

open look kids often had. A darkness lingered in the back of the child's gaze.

"I need help."

This isn't social services. He quelled the quick retort that came to mind.

When did I get so fucking hardened to life?

He knew when, he knew exactly when. The day a kid that should have been in kindergarten picked his pocket.

"What do you need help with?" He regarded the urchin's tattered clothing, the holes in the jeans.

"My mom's being booked."

A kid that young shouldn't even know the words *being booked*; he sure as hell shouldn't be saying his mother was being booked.

"What for?"

"Honest, Officer. She was getting us a tree."

He didn't need anyone to translate that one for him. She was being booked for stealing. "What did she take?" Take was such a nicer word, especially for one that young.

"A Christmas tree." He wrung his hands, caught himself, shoved them deep into jean pockets. "It was my fault. I told her I hated her. That she never gave me a Christmas. That I wished she'd never had me."

Ouch. He nodded. "Who brought you here?"

"I followed the police car."

Isaac closed his eyes against the image of the little

one running behind a patrol vehicle while his mother was being taken away. He opened them.

"Don't call social services, please. I'll just run away. I want my mom to come home. Take me instead, it's my fault, after all. Take me to jail." He held out his hands, wrists together, ready to be cuffed.

That moment Isaac saw Cadence's face, heard her words: *It's black and white for you, just like that?*

"Fu—" He clamped his mouth shut. Maybe the curvy brunette had a point after all?

He pushed his chair away from the desk and stood next to the kid, towering above the little man who'd learned way too much at too early of an age.

"Let's find your mother."

Isaac's morning was spent finding the boy's mother, having her released, then taking them on a shopping excursion, a trip very different from the one he'd had with Cadence.

He'd provided them with a tree and presents for beneath the tree. The little boy once more was a child, not a miniature man who knew too much, too early.

The kid wrapped his arms around Isaac's legs, thanking him.

The shine of tears were the mother's thank you.

He'd handed the woman his card. "Call me Monday. We'll see if we can't help you find a job."

The tears had flowed.

Not a bad day, after all. Now he was meeting Ky—time to get the operation going. That damned cat burglar was getting the best of Isaac, and the perfect ending to Isaac's day would be to close the case.

"Got them?" Isaac glanced at Ky's empty hands.

Ky patted his pocket. "Got them. Did you set out the bait?"

"Trap's set." Isaac knew his smile was grim, but no one was more ready for this ordeal to be over. The thought another shifter was fooling him didn't sit well.

"You sound like you're hunting." Laken watched them from the couch.

"That's exactly what I'm doing." Isaac glanced at his watch. "I don't want to delay getting there. I need to be set up."

The story had been carefully planted with sources in the criminal world. A mansion the NYPD had seized in a drug bust was the place he'd set a trap for the perp.

Again, Isaac was working outside the purview of the NYPD and without backup. Again, Ky had given him shit about it, but this was something Isaac had to do, and he wanted to do it alone. His bear growled in agreement.

The house was two stories tall, surrounded by trees on a moonless night. It was a cat burglar's dream.

Except he'd make sure the cat burglar got a surprise. He'd catch her.

He'd told Ky he wanted to handle it alone. Being the baby brother of a clan of alpha polar bears hadn't always been easy. He wanted to follow in Jonah's footsteps and become a part of Unit 13, but he didn't want his brothers getting him there.

Isaac stretched sore muscles. He'd positioned himself in an armoire in the room on the second floor that held the safe. The door was open a crack, placed perfectly so he was facing the safe.

Where the hell is she?

Had the sources not passed the information along? Was the perp not coming? It was almost four o'clock, and she was notorious for striking before four. He found himself admiring the cat burglar even though he would put her in cuffs. She was disciplined and successful, even though her success was in illegal practices.

He set the tranq pistol down and flexed his fingers, careful not to let them pop, because a shifter would hear that from a good distance away.

Come on. Come on.

He paused.

There.

Thank goodness he'd used hunter's block himself.

A shadow entered the room. She was fully clad in black, from her mask to the tips of her black boots. She moved with grace and stealth, her back to him. If it were any other time, he'd pause to admire the curves on her, except…

She was a criminal.

And mostly…

He couldn't get another set of curves off his mind.

Cadence.

He pushed the thoughts away. He needed to have his mind fully on this mission. There'd be time to think of Cadence later. There was Christmas with his family, after all.

Her back still to him, the perp lifted the black mask off her head and shoved it into a back pocket. She took one of two paintings off the wall, revealing the safe.

It was a different painting than the one Isaac had told the informant about. He'd wanted to see if she'd done her homework.

She had.

He was mesmerized by the confidence in her movements. As soon as she had the bag full of cash and jewelry, he would hit her with the tranq. He wanted her to be beyond denial of her dastardly acts.

Just as she closed the safe, her backpack full of loot, he raised the pistol, took careful aim for her thigh, and pulled the trigger back slowly.

Except she sneezed, and her body flinched.

AT THE PRECISE moment she sneezed, Cade heard a slight pop, then felt a sting, like bumping into a cactus. The next thing she heard was the sound of something bouncing off the wall and landing on the floor.

A quick glance verified it was a dart.

A fucking dart? A tranq?

Are you fucking kidding me?

Who would...?

How would they...?

She was ready to whirl around and determine who and where her attacker was when a slight wooziness hit her. She had to get the hell out of here, because she had no idea how potent it was, and how much had gotten into her. And if there was a second one coming.

Oh, shit. Not a second one.

Her hand hooked the backpack as she made a dash for the door, sprinted through and turned left. Then she realized her mistake. She needed to turn right.

Fuck.

She ran into a room and closed and locked the door behind her. She had seconds before whoever shot her would find and open the door.

She opened the window. She could handle this

jump. Of course she could. She shook her head to clear it.

Damn wooziness. Everything was out of focus and she was seeing double.

I'd already be out by now if that damned thing had stuck in me instead of glancing off.

Maybe she had a chance. She shifted quickly, grabbed the full backpack between her teeth and leaped through the window. Her panther legs felt like they were lead-filled. She plummeted to the ground, trying to arch her body, but instead of her usual graceful actions, she moved as if she were in quicksand.

That thought didn't last long. She crashed into the ground, one front leg popping. Behind her, in the room she'd just leaped out of, she could hear the door giving in to a kick.

She rose to her paws as quickly as she could and ran for the cover the trees offered a few yards away. She'd just entered the thicket when she turned and looked at the window.

Isaac.

Why am I not surprised?

She watched him looking into the trees and wondered if he'd come looking for her.

Do I really want to find out? A panther can outrun a bear. I need to get the hell out of here.

She couldn't stay in panther form for long, though.

That was all she needed, to have someone see a black panther running around loose.

She shook her head to clear it.

Isaac vanished from the window.

Time to get the hell out of here.

She walked for what felt like forever in her tranquilizer-laden state, then stopped and leaned against a tree.

Fucking tranq. Fucking Isaac.

That was a cheap stunt—hitting her with a tranq.

She sank against the trunk, slowly lowering herself to the ground. Her eyes closed, heavy with drowsiness.

He couldn't follow her. She'd left no scent.

Thank God for hunter's block.

She could rest here, just for a second, until the fuzziness vanished.

Isaac was in a state of shock. He was running on autopilot, going through the routine of hunting for the criminal but a part of him was somewhere else.

Surely he hadn't seen what he'd thought he was seeing. It couldn't have been, but then again…

No, that makes no damned sense at all.

When the perp had turned her head just after the tranq had clipped her, her profile…

No. It couldn't be. A part of him refused to accept it, even though he knew what he'd seen.

That was Cadence's profile.

He'd run to the window to look for her but she was long gone. The tranq hadn't done a very good job.

He took a deep breath and picked up the scent of her blood. The dart had nicked her enough to make her bleed and had left particles of her scent in the air.

He breathed again, searching for what he knew would be there.

There it is.

He'd put scent on the cash. Nothing she'd have noticed. It was too subtle. But he'd made sure it was enough of a scent for him to follow.

He headed down toward the thicket he knew she'd gone into. He didn't have to witness it to know she'd shifted and slipped into the trees. He'd follow the scent of the money until he found her.

He let out a deep breath.

Then what?

Yeah, then what? Tell the woman that he couldn't imagine living without that she'd have to turn herself in?

His bear growled.

I know. I know she's not the criminal type, but how do you reconcile that with what I just caught her doing?

His bear snarled.

Fine, we caught her doing. Hey. Don't get pissed at me. And this fated mates thing, that's your deal.

Isaac knew he wasn't fooling his bear. He'd fallen hard for the curvy brunette with the flashing dark eyes. Isaac made his way to the woods and began to tail her on foot through the trees. Soon enough the trees would lead to the park the property backed up to. Then it would lead to apartments. Then...

What if she got into her car and went home? Then the only way to prove she was the culprit was to catch her with the goods he'd planted.

At least he didn't have to worry about getting those back into the evidence locker. He hadn't borrowed them from the department. This time, he had another source.

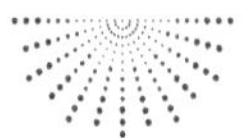

A hit to her still-sensitive wrist ripped through Cade's semi-conscious state. She jerked awake just in time to see a boot pulling back to nudge her again.

The boot had come within inches of her arm when she grabbed it and yanked hard, pulling the person attached to it to the ground. He was young, barely out of his teens, wearing a denim jacket and jeans, with a beanie pulled over a mess of hair.

She sprang up, her faculties mostly back, though she remained a little shaky.

"What the fuck, bitch." Another one, who could have been a brother to the one on the ground, approached her.

"I don't want trouble." She stammered the words out, stumbling over the syllables.

How long had she been out? It was still dark outside, without the slightest hint of daylight.

I need to get the hell out of here before the cops show up and open this bag.

She reached for her bag.

It was gone.

"Looking for this?" A third guy popped up, raising her backpack, tossing it to his left.

"That's mine."

"I don't think so," a fourth guy said, catching the backpack. He was heavier, older, and his face had a hardened look to it.

Looks like he's the boss.

Being a shifter didn't mean she could kick everyone's ass when she was in human form.

And shifting right now is out of the question.

"What's in here?"

So they hadn't opened it. She took a deep breath. "My medicine."

"Oh, medicine…" The older guy winked at his friends. "A little weed?"

"No." She reached for the bag.

He pulled back, and she stepped closer. If she could get it, maybe she could make a run for it? She couldn't take all four of them on, especially not the way she felt.

Hands grabbed her arm from behind. Another pair grabbed her other arm.

She tried to shake them off. "Let me go." Her

warning sounded more like a growl. Her panther was becoming furious. A shift would be inevitable if they didn't leave her alone. She wouldn't be able to control her feline from coming to her defense.

That's not exactly what I want, shifting into my panther while I'm surrounded by people.

Not at all.

She struggled against their grip on her arms.

"Bitch, quit," one of them hissed at her.

"Let me go!"

She heard a noise, one she knew all too well because Uncle Ramon used to have one: a switchblade being ejected from its housing.

The leader had the deadly glinting object in his right hand.

If she could kick him just right, if she could…

Who was she kidding? She was outnumbered and still not 100 percent after that damned tranquilizer dart.

Damn Isaac Romanoff.

The leader tossed the backpack to the guy who'd thrown it to him and then flipped the switchblade from one hand to the other. "Give me what I want and you don't have to die."

"You already have what you want. You took my backpack."

Thank God they haven't opened it yet.

Cade braced herself; she'd have to fight.

"You know what I mean, *puta*."

"I don't think you should be calling the lady names."

That voice.

Isaac.

Relief flooded Cade, except it was quickly replaced by fear—not a fear of the thugs as much as a fear that he knew who'd just robbed that house. He had to know. It couldn't be an accident he was here.

"Who you think *you* are?" the leader asked, indicating to the men holding Cade that they should approach Isaac.

Isaac saving her from them would mean her ending up behind bars. Who was she supposed to root for? Him or them? And was there a chance she could make it out of this?

Only if he's dead.

Her panther's sentiments echoed inside her mind.

Isaac's steely gaze took the leader's measure without forfeiting the attention he was giving the other two. When they rushed him, he sidestepped one and deftly delivered a kick that knocked the man to the ground on his side, several feet away.

The second man glanced at the leader, as if he was second-guessing the wisdom of his decision to have them attack Isaac.

Isaac didn't wait; he stepped into the man's space. The man raised his arms, fists ready and aimed for Isaac's head. One swift move from Isaac took him out of harm's way, his hand dropped, and quicker than the man's eyes would have registered it, he delivered a kick to the man's leg, sending him tumbling to the ground, groaning in agony.

The third man dropped Cade's backpack and picked up a branch as thick as his arm. He swung it, approaching Isaac.

"You're dead." The leader's voice was a low hiss. He rushed toward Isaac.

Cade sidestepped as if she were avoiding the husky leader, and as soon as his back was to her, she rushed forward, aiming her fists for his kidneys.

At the same time she wondered what the hell she was thinking, getting involved in this and saving the man who was going to ruin her life.

She pummeled the thug's back with blows. The switchblade-wielding thug turned around, and before Cade could react, she felt the cold steel of his weapon sliding into her stomach.

She gasped.

Shock made her freeze.

She clutched her stomach, to find blood pouring between her fingers.

The sound that came out of her mouth was her panther's voice.

A low roar came from the left. A huge polar bear, white fur gleaming in the darkness, swatted the man in front of him out of the way with one swipe, and ripped into the leader with massive claws, severing arteries and leaving the man to bleed to death.

Isaac wanted to yell, to scream, but he could do none of that. He'd watched as the woman he loved jumped on the bastard's back… and then the man had turned and shoved that switchblade deep into her belly.

She was looking down at her stomach when he shifted, unable to contain the emotions that pushed him into that shift. His bear roared in pain. He struck the men quickly, killing one immediately and leaving the other to die slowly.

He shifted back into his skin. "Jesus, Cade."

She swayed back, then toward him. He leaped forward and grabbed her just as her eyes rolled back in her head.

"God. No."

Hope wilted in him; she couldn't lose consciousness. Not now. She needed to shift into her panther so she could heal.

"Fuck."

The backpack. It was evidence that would put her in jail.

He swooped down and picked it up.

Then he carried her toward the mansion they'd left not long ago.

CHAPTER FIFTEEN

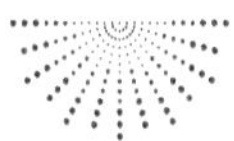

Cade woke in her panther form. She knew this without even opening her eyes. She didn't remember shifting. She tried to remember what she did last, but her memory was fuzzy and her head felt full of cotton.

Her panther on full alert; she opened her eyes slowly. She was greeted by a mountain of white fur. She recognized immediately the fur belonged to Isaac, his scent permeated her senses, filling her lungs.

Her eyes focused, studied her surroundings. Not her apartment, had to be his.

She looked at him again. He was covered in blood.

The recent events came crashing down around her head. Her thwarted escape. The thugs. The backpack. The attack. The stabbing.

She leapt to her feet, shifted quickly and soundlessly, and scanned the room for her backpack.

Her panther noticed a change in his heartbeat. Isaac was awake. Cade glanced down. He'd fixed her with a piercing stare, shifting while he rose to his feet.

"You're better." He straightened his clothing, which had become askew, as clothing tended to, after a shift.

"You saved my life." She tried to feel appreciation, except she knew he'd saved her to put her in prison. *May as well not have saved me.*

"You saved mine, too." He opened the closet door, took out her backpack. "You could have lost yours saving me."

"It's risky to fight in public, shifting could lead to witnesses." She was babbling, she knew it but she didn't want to talk about her backpack. She wanted to pretend not to see it, not to be the one he was hunting.

"There were no witnesses. I made sure of that." His face was grim.

She knew that had to be difficult for him; he was a law enforcement officer, after all. "I'm sorry I put you in that position."

"I did what had to be done."

For me.

And now he'd have to put her in prison.

She'd go easily, without a struggle, without complicating his life anymore.

"I understand. I'd like to make this as easy as possible. I don't want my sisters to have to deal with any of the fallout."

"Will you tell me why you did these jobs?"

She shook her head. What did it matter? Knowing why she did it wouldn't keep him from doing his job.

"It doesn't matter." She fiddled with her shirt, her fingers playing with the tear the blade had left in the fabric.

"Maybe it matters to me."

"Your world is black and white. I don't operate in a black and white world. I see varying degree of shades."

"Try me."

Something in his tone caught her attention. She glanced up. There was something in his gaze. She couldn't peg the expression but something told her he'd changed. This was not the same man she'd argued with in the deli.

She took a seat on the corner of the bed.

An hour and what seemed like a bucket full of tears later, she'd told him all about Ignacio. How Ignacio's stepfather had killed him. How she'd sought retribution by allowing her panther to kill the stepfather. How every penny she stole was purposed for building Ignacio's Place.

He was nodding. Somewhere during the telling, he'd sat next to her, and now his arm was around her, offering her solace.

"You're amazing," he said.

"But I still belong in jail," she finished the thought for him.

"I didn't say that. I didn't say that at all."

"What's different? Where's the black and white guy I used to know?"

"Let's say he's seen the other side."

She nodded, encouraging him to keep talking.

He continued, "Maybe there should be special circumstances…"

"Do tell."

"You'll have to return the stuff you stole."

It felt like the air had been crushed out of her like a can of soda.

"I can't." How could he say that? "After everything I told you, do you really think I can stop the project?"

"No one said anything about you stopping the project."

"It takes funding. I can help with that."

Her laugh was humorless. "Police officers don't make a lot of money."

"True. But there's my trust fund."

Was he being funny? Because this wasn't much of a joking matter for her. "I'm not amused."

"Seriously. You've seen my uncle's place. I know you realize they aren't hurting. My dad was Mikhail's brother. When my father and my mother…" He shook his head. "Let's just say there's a trust fund with a good amount of money in it. Enough to replenish what you've stolen and still fulfill your dreams for Ignacio's Place. It's just sitting there, earning interest. I never touch it. None of us do."

She sat back, tucked her knees beneath her chin and hugged her shins, staring at him. "You'd do that?"

"I would."

She raised a brow. "No strings?"

"I didn't say that."

She jumped to a stand, fuming. "I knew it. What's it going to be? Jail time?"

"You spend Christmas Eve with me."

"We're already going to your aunt's on Christmas day at eleven."

"Yeah, but that's not what I want. I want Christmas Eve."

"That's it? That's tomorrow."

"Give the money back. Give me Christmas Eve. I'll fund Ignacio's Place."

"And arresting me?"

He took a deep breath. His chest expanded, so wide, so very sexy, even in a rumpled shirt. Beneath the fabric were abs, flexed and rippled. Cadence turned away, because if she kept looking at him, she'd forget he was the enemy. An enemy who meant way too much to her.

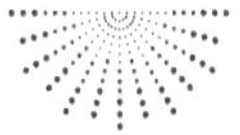

Isaac was conflicted, Cadence asked about arresting her, and he hadn't answered. All he'd given her was "I'll pick you up at five."

He couldn't do it. He couldn't arrest the woman he loved, the panther his bear called mate.

He'd gone to visit Uncle Mikhail, laid out the barest of facts. Told his uncle he was in love with a woman who'd done the wrong thing for all the right reason.

Aunt Miriam had stepped into Mikhail's study, and found the two of them deep in conversation, then slipped out.

"You're like a son to me," Uncle Mikhail had said.

"And you like a father to all of us."

Mikhail tapped on the dark wood desk top in his office.

"What does your bear say?"

Isaac toyed with a paperweight on his uncle's desk.

"You didn't give the bear a voice? Look, Isaac, I've never counseled you on how you treat your bear. I know it hasn't been an easy time for you and you've clashed over the years, but your bear is a part of you. You should let the bear have a say."

My bear wants her. My bear calls her his mate already.

Ky didn't need to ask the bear, the bear would tell him to forget everything, to cast aside his ethics.

"My bear's advice is tainted."

Mikhail's eyes narrowed. "I don't think you meant that the way it sounded."

"My bear's opinion is jaded. Is that better?"

In Isaac's mind, his bear growled.

"What does your heart say?"

"That's where things get tricky. My heart agrees with my bear."

The doorbell rang.

"I think you need to sort this out on your own." Mikhail stood and walked toward the office door. "I'll get the door."

So basically I have the same dilemma I had when I walked in.

His bear snarled.

He had to pick up Cadence, and he needed to figure out what he would do.

He stepped out of his uncle's office and almost ran into Laken.

"Hey." He looked around. "Where's Ky?"

"He's at home."

She looked so much like Cadence it made his heart ache to think of what was expected of him.

She leaned against the door, her face pale.

"Are you okay?" Isaac took her by the arm, leading her toward a chair. Her limp, normally barely noticeable, was pronounced.

"I'm fine." She dabbed at her temple, where she had a light sheen of perspiration.

"I don't think you are."

"I can't discuss it with you. Not right now."

Shit. She knows. Cadence must have told her. "Does this involve Cadence?"

She gave him a look. "No. Why would it? What's wrong with Cade?"

"Nothing. I—" Now what the hell was he supposed to say. He spied Aunt Miriam approaching, his perfect chance to escape. "I have to go. See you Christmas day."

She gave him an odd look as he slipped off.

ISAAC PACED the lobby of Cadence's apartment. He was going to pick her up but he hadn't told her what they were doing and he hadn't told her his decision about arresting her.

Or not arresting her.

"Why didn't you come up?" Cadence's voice came from behind him.

"I haven't been here long."

"Long enough to wear a pattern in the flooring." She planted hands on hips. "I've been watching you."

Shit. She'd been watching him pace.

CADE FELT BAD FOR ISAAC. She knew she'd put him in an uncomfortable position.

What about my position.

True. She was facing incarceration, but that was her choice. Isaac hadn't done anything to deserve being in this situation.

She let him help her into the car without asking where they were going. She'd already asked him for enough. He was funding Ignacio's Place.

A bit later Isaac surprised her by parking in an area that was dilapidated and of questionable safety. Cade cast him a sideways glance, burning to ask why he'd brought her here. The stoops were occupied by discarded furniture pieces and denizens whose breath frosted in the cold air.

Every other streetlight was out, and as luck would

have it, the one near them was out. Not that it mattered, thank goodness for shifter vision.

Isaac exited and opened the door for her. He led her to the back of his sedan and popped the trunk with the remote.

"Give me a hand?" He indicated one of three boxes. He picked one up. "Stack that one on this one. And can you grab the smallest one?"

Cade was still perturbed. "Sure."

Four flights later, Isaac set the boxes down and knocked on a door.

A kid answered, not much older than Ignacio was when he died. "Officer Romanoff! Look, Mom!" The boy flung the door wide, revealing a too-thin woman with tired eyes and creases where a smile should have been.

She regarded Isaac with suspiciousness. "Are you taking me in?" Then she noticed Cade and frowned. "Social services. I should have known." She shook her head, disbelief and disappointment prevalent in her sloping shoulders.

"Nope." Isaac picked up the boxes and walked in. "Not here in any official capacity. This is my—This is Cadence. She's a teacher."

Cade gave him a double take. What was he going to say? She'd have to ask. And if she was his *anything* then it didn't seem he'd be carting her off to prison, did it? Or was he thinking she'd do her time and he'd wait.

What the hell am I thinking? We've kissed, nothing more. Her panther snarled.

Okay, okay, maybe there's more.

"So why are you here?" The woman's voice hadn't lost its tinge of distrust.

"Cadence, this is Mary and that's Eric."

"Nice to meet you." Cadence kept her tone light.

"What's in the boxes, Officer Romanoff?" Eric jumped up and down. "Look, Cadence." Eric grabbed her hand and pulled her from the short hallway into the living room. "See the tree and the presents? Officer Romanoff gave those to us."

Cadence glanced at Isaac.

He pointedly avoided her gaze, instead, telling Eric, "Isaac, not Officer Romanoff. I'm off duty."

"I didn't think you were ever off duty," Cadence hissed the words low, inaudible to human hearing.

Isaac cut his eyes her way, gave her a quirked eyebrow.

"So this isn't an official visit?" Mary's shoulders slumped even more, this time in visible relief.

"Nope. Just brought you a few extra things I had at my place." He set the boxes on the table.

Cade put hers next to them.

Mary pulled the box open, poked through it. "These things still have tags on them."

"Yeah, uh…" Isaac cleared his throat. "I never got around to using them."

Cade's panther scented the lie. She smirked. Isaac gave her a dirty look over Mary's head. Cade feigned interest in the items Mary was ooohing and ahhhing over.

"Not everything's black and white," Isaac said.

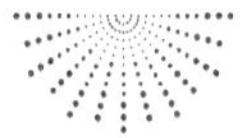

An evening of setting up Mary's kitchen and jazzing up Eric's bedroom ended quickly. Cade settled into Isaac's car, the heat from the vents warming chilled limbs.

"They didn't have the heat on." It hadn't occurred to her before.

"Not sure they can afford it. Mary's out of work. I'll help her line something up on Monday." He told her about his meeting with Eric and the circumstances of Mary's arrest for stealing a Christmas tree.

"That's nice of you." She chewed on her lip, Mary's arrest made the subject of her incarceration prevalent in her mind again. She pushed it away. "What happened to the black and white guy?"

"He's seen a different perspective."

"Isaac. I know you're struggling, and we're pretty

close to related, what with my sister and your brother being mates…" She heaved a sigh. "I'm going to turn myself in. I don't want you to be the one who has to take the heat from our families. Except it means you won't get the credit." She tried to force a reconciliatory smile to her face. "At least, you won't get the blame, right?"

Isaac pulled the car into her garage, nosed the vehicle into her spot, shifted into park, turned to face her. "No."

He opened the car door, got out, opened hers.

"But…"

"No." He strode toward the elevator, pressed the button.

She powerwalked to keep up with him. "Stop. Listen to me. If you turn me in, then you're going to create a problem with our families. I'll just go in quietly, turn myself in, and ta-da! You're off the hook."

The door opened. He entered the elevator. She took a step in his direction. "Thanks for walking me inside."

Before she could take a second step he'd reached for her, his large hand encircling her arm, he pulled her into the elevator.

The door closed behind her. His eyes held her prisoner. "Listen." He let go of her arm, scrubbed his face, the days' growth scratchy.

She leaned against the shiny metal wall. "Okay." She crossed her arms.

"I can't. I can't have you turning yourself in." He looked away, pushed the button for her floor.

Her stomach lurched and it felt like the temperature dropped a thousand degrees. *He means he wants to take me in himself.* "So the alternative is?"

The elevator dinged. A crowd stood in front of her, blocking the way, but she couldn't concentrate on them. She stepped out, her vision blurred with tears of helplessness.

What the fuck. I don't cry.

The crowd parted around her and entered the elevator, swarming on.

"Cadence."

She didn't turn around fully. She didn't want him to see her crying, even if it wasn't tears of sadness or self-pity. Cadence shook her head. "No."

"Hold the door open," he said to someone on the elevator. She swiped at her face, composed her expression and turned to face him.

He was trapped by a baby stroller.

"Wait," was the last thing she heard him say as the door closed.

That's when she noticed—*this isn't even my fucking floor.* She was two floors down from her floor.

"Fuck."

And that's exactly where he was going. Her floor. She didn't feel like talking to him. Didn't want to listen to his excuses about why he was taking her in personally.

She crossed to the stairway and took the steps down two at a time, exited to the lobby and headed out the front door. She didn't want to see Isaac Romanoff.

God. I have to face it. The man I'm in love with is turning me into the cops. Hell, he's not turning me in, he's the cop arresting me.

She wandered for more than an hour, then she'd come back in, made sure his car was gone before going up to her apartment.

She'd still have to deal with him tomorrow. Unless she could avoid the Romanoffs for Christmas.

I'll call Laken, tell her I can't make it. That I've got a tummy thing going on.

That would do it.

She slipped the key into the lock, opened the door, then closed it behind her.

Carina wasn't there. The place was quiet.

Except…

She paused.

The hairs on the back of her neck stood up.

"You never let me finish what I was saying."

She jumped.

Isaac.

Her panther shifted part way, her teeth erupting, claws erupting. She snarled.

"Easy," Isaac said. "It's just me." He stepped out of the shadows.

She reshifted to her human. "You…" She couldn't say *scared me*, because she wasn't scared, but her alarms certainly went off enough to cause her panther to surge for a shift. "You caught me off guard."

"I didn't mean to. Where have you been? I've been concerned."

"I'm sorry. I saw you tried to call." *At least a dozen times since I left you in the elevator.* "I was thinking. What did you want to say?" *That you were going to put me in prison?*

His eyes narrowed, a flash appeared in their depths, then his lips pursed.

God, so very fucking kissable. She tore her gaze away from his lips, concentrated on his eyes.

"What do you mean what did I want to say?" His tone had an underlying steel quality to it that vibrated throughout her body, sending waves of desire coursing clear to the very tip of her nerve endings.

How the hell does he affect me this way? she thought back to a conversation she'd had with Laken before she and Ky had left for overseas. Laken had told her that a part of her had always known Ky was for her.

When Cade had pressed her for more, Laken said it was a combination of her heart and her panther, or so she thought. She'd said that the emotions were stronger than any she'd ever felt.

That's exactly what Isaac does to me. Isaac. The man who would put cuffs on her in the next few moments.

She opened her mouth to speak but nothing came out. She swallowed. "I'll only ask one thing. Just one favor. Please let me have Christmas with my sisters. After that, I'm yours."

He leaned against the breakfast bar, thick arms crossed over a chest that narrowed to a delicious vee.

Her panther chuffed a sound of appreciation. Cade agreed, completely.

"So you're all mine if I give you Christmas day with your sisters. Just like that?"

That voice. So deep. So sexy. So… all man. All shifter. All alpha.

A surge of reactions throughout her body.

Another chuff from her panther.

We both need to relax. You and I know that's not what he meant or how he meant it.

She nodded. "Yes. All yours. To take me in to the police station. You can get the credit for the capture. Get your promotion. Live happily ever after." *And all that other shit.*

She'd barely finished her sentence, hadn't completely finished her thought when he moved with more speed than she would have expected from a polar bear shifter.

It's not like I know any other polar bear shifters—just him. And his family.

He stood in front of her, breathing her air, his body in her personal space, reminding her how powerful he was, his strong jaw jutting in a display that said he was angry. His teeth clenched so tightly, her shifter hearing picked up the sound of their grinding.

It was a struggle, having this man she wanted badly close to her. So close, and yet so very far, considering what he planned for her.

She looked up at him, his diamantine gaze piercing straight through her, as if he could read her very thoughts, essence, and even her panther's emotions.

He puffed out a long breath, surrounding her in a blend of scents, eau de Isaac, piney woods, earthy, all man.

He stepped closer, leaving nary an inch between them. She felt her heartbeat sync with his, the pounding of her pulse so loud it filled her head.

When he put his hands on her hips, though his touch was light, she felt like she was surrounded by a safety harness. The warmth of his flesh traveled through the fabric of her clothing.

A moisture she couldn't have controlled if she'd wanted to responded to his touch.

"You're mine to take, but not in. I couldn't live with myself if I took you in for trying to create Ignacio's Place any more than I could have let Mary go to jail."

"What? No. You can't do that. I know what being

with InterForce means to you. Laken said it's your dream."

"Dreams change. Better dreams come along." A slight tilt to his lips yielded a little smile, but his eyes held an emotion she wasn't sure about.

"No, Isaac. I can't let you do that."

"You can't stop me. I have a backup plan, anyway."

"Meaning…?"

"I'll do contract work for InterForce."

She narrowed her eyes. "I'm not sure."

He growled, lifted her off her feet, pulled her against his body with such intensity the breath left her body. His lips claimed hers with a hot and undeniable possession.

She boldly snaked her arms around his neck, pulled herself tighter against him while her lips pressed on his with a desperation she'd never have thought she felt.

Not she. Not Cadence Araya who'd never needed anyone, who'd fended for herself for far too long.

Between them, his desire was a rod of steel, insistent with need. Lips still locked, he swung her upward and carried her toward her bedroom, shouldering the slightly ajar door completely open.

He released her, a fierce desire shining in his eyes. She pressed a finger to her swollen lip.

"Be sure, Cadence. Be very sure. I'm not going to let you walk out of this room an unbonded woman. If you yield to me now, you yield forever. You become mine."

She stood on her toes, pinning him with her gaze. There were two hostages in this. Two takers. Two givers. It would be mutual. All the way. "As do you."

Isaac regarded her. "I wouldn't have it any other way, cat burglar. I want nothing less than all of you. You'll get no less from me."

"Forever," she cautioned him.

"Always."

Isaac ached for her with a passion unprecedented for him. Once he'd allowed his bear to fully become one with him on this, once he'd yielded to himself and the truth, an avalanche of restrained needs and emotions flowed through him with the fury of a natural disaster. He couldn't have anything less than all of this woman.

His cock was hard, watching this woman who'd give as much as she'd take and match him in everything he ever did.

She was his fated mate. There was no way around that. In his mind, his bear released a roar that sealed their fate.

My mate. His bear snarled agreement.

Her caramel colored skin was infused with the pink flush of desire. Her lips swollen a dusky pink from their kiss. Her breaths were hard, heaving her breasts, leaving him yearning to rip her clothing off.

He fought to regain control, but couldn't. Yielding to his bear, he unsheathed a claw and sliced through the fabric cleanly. He let his gaze rake over her body with a slowness that built a crescendo of desire within him.

Dark rosy nipples puckered in the room's air, jutting forward, tempting him to touch. Her full breasts rose and fell, a lighter caramel color than her face, their rising and falling increased and he realized this was from the effect of his gaze on her body.

"Fuck." He released the word in an exhale, and hadn't even realized he'd said it out loud until she shivered.

"Isaac." Her voice was sex-hoarse. She reached out boldly, pulled him from his pants, running her fingers over the length of his shaft.

His breath caught, burning his lungs while her fingers worked their magic, trailing their way back and forth along his cock. When she wrapped her fingers around his girth, a tiny explosion in his mind yielded a drop of pleasure on the slit of his mushroom head.

She thumbed it, rubbing the dewy moisture into the head, turning the pleasure of it into an exquisite pain of need that made his cock throb.

He cupped her breast with one hand while he slid another hand between her legs, to the place he wanted to bury his cock. He parted her folds.

"You're wet for me."

Cadence arched her body toward his, her breast filling his hand while her clit pressed against his hand.

He lowered his head, taking a pearlized nipple into his mouth, drawing it in, sucking fiercely while she rocked on his hand, pressing him closer and closer to slipping a finger into that dark delightful place.

She released a moan that pushed him over the edge.

He pushed her onto the bed, and traveled his hands over her quivering body. He laid a concentration of licks, kisses, and flicks on her nipples while he journeyed lower, taking his sweet time getting to the apex he wanted while she trembled beneath his attentions. He rained kisses on her stomach, over each hip, over the downy dainty treasure trail.

He curtailed his desire to take her while he neared the tiny triangle of trimmed hair. Cadence squirmed, her body arching upward, offering herself to him.

He lingered over her mound, inhaling the scent of her, the sex of her.

This woman, his mate, his everything.

He spread her folds, drenched with the results of her desire. He surveyed the bounty of her offerings, her dark pink clit swollen.

He dipped his head, taking the nub into his mouth, drawing it in, sucking, careful not to push her too far too fast. Her body tightened, hips rising.

She laced her fingers into his hair, her nails digging into his scalp the moment his tongue flicked her clit.

She brought his head downward, brought her hips up while he plunged his tongue into her loveliness. She rode his mouth, grinding against his face, giving both of them pleasure as he found a rhythm. Catching him off guard, she released an orgasm into his mouth. He lapped the juices from her slit.

She thrust upward with a groan, soaking both of them again. Isaac moved up and over her, his composure fled the moment she'd climaxed in his mouth.

Now he wanted one thing. Her. All of her. Claiming her. Bonding her. Making her his forever.

CADE'S BODY erupted in a myriad of sensations brought on by his lips, his fingers, his mouth, his very presence.

His cock nudged at her entrance for a brief second before he pressed in with a thrust that forced the breath from her lungs.

Her moan merged with a groan, becoming one sound as his cock claimed her body with the same passion he claimed her heart and his bear had claimed her panther. A swell of pain shot through her as he filled her. Her muscles spread to accommodate him, taking all of him in.

Her body curved to meet every thrust, taking him in deep, then missing him as he pulled out, only to fill her again. She clawed at his back, seeking purchase from the passion that overwhelmed her. His fingers gripped into her ass, pulling her so close there was no space between them.

A wave started at the very core of her being, undulating outward, carrying her on a tide of pleasure, pushing her further and further toward a place she'd not be able to return from.

She wrapped her legs around his waist. "Isaac," she moaned. "Help me, please."

His eyes focused on her face, his own features contorted by desire.

"Tell me what you want."

"I want you. Always."

He drew back, almost pulling out completely. "Woman. You. Have. Me."

With one huge thrust, he was ensconced deep within, his hotness spreading within like liquid fire as he bit down on her neck, sharp incisors bonding them.

She opened her mouth to scream the agony of pleasure and pain taking her away when Isaac's mouth covered hers.

He propped himself up on one arm, careful not to crush her while his body blanketed hers with safety and a bond that would transcend time.

Hours later, when she woke, he was still next to her, watching her with those eyes that never seemed to miss a thing.

"You knew, didn't you? Knew it was me?"

"My bear did. He's not…" Isaac released a long breath. "He doesn't always confide everything to me. At least, he didn't used to. I'm hoping things are better from this point on."

"When did you figure out it, then?"

"When you took off your mask, at the mansion."

"Could you have ever—" Cade couldn't bring herself to say the words.

He traced circle patterns on her hips, making her lose her train of thought.

His fingertips froze. "Turned you in?"

She nodded.

"Never. Even if you weren't mine." His eyes flashed his bear's, a golden white glow.

Tears burned the bridge of her nose, only they weren't tears of helplessness.

"You owe me Christmas tomorrow."

"You can have all my Christmases. Forever."

EPILOGUE

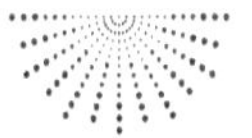

The Romanoffs and the Araya sisters were seated at the dinner table. One seat was notably empty. Jonah's.

Miriam Romanoff had invited another friend, Fiona, who was scated across from Jonah's vacant spot.

Christmas dinner—traditionally so—was ham and turkey.

Miriam had placed Cadence's seat across from Isaac's. Isaac gave his aunt the eye. "So you knew?"

"Maybe you *were* the last to know she was meant for you." Mikhail Romanoff boomed.

Cadence caught Isaac's eye and turned a delicious shade of pink.

"So how's the case?" Aunt Miriam's eyes twinkled.

Cadence looked down.

Isaac frowned at his aunt. Surely she didn't know about that, too, did she?

Nah, she couldn't have.

A part of him wasn't convinced she didn't, though she glanced away, not confirming the answer to the question he tried to pose with his eyes.

"It's slow going," Isaac responded.

Cadence looked up, a small smile on her face. Isaac gave her a wink.

"So what's the news?" he asked Laken and Ky. "You said you had something to tell us."

"Not until Jonah's here," Ky said.

"Has Jonah called?" Miriam asked Mikhail.

"Not me he hasn't. Anyone heard from Jonah?"

"I'm pretty sure I'm the last one he'd call," Fiona said. A blonde beauty, as curvy as the Araya sisters, she grimaced. "He probably found out I'm here. That's why he's not."

"Oh, my. I don't think he harbors ill will toward you, Fiona. It's been a while since…"

Since…

Aunt Miriam didn't say since when, but Isaac knew. Since Fiona broke his brother's heart.

He was pretty sure Jonah would have skipped if he knew Fi was here. But none of them had known. So where was his wayward brother?

"Maybe he's not coming," Ky said. "Could be he's caught in a case? Shall we share the news?"

Ky rose, held his hand out for Laken to stand.

Her cheeks pinked. "We're having a baby." She put her hands over her stomach that showed no signs of a baby yet.

Cadence and Carina both simultaneously squealed, jumped up and ran around the table to embrace their sister.

Isaac hugged his brother. "Congratulations."

Miriam's hand was over the perfect *O* her mouth made. Tears streamed down her face.

"I'm so happy."

Even Mikhail Romanoff, never at a loss for words, had nothing to say, just beamed happiness. Finally, he said. "I wish your father and mother were here, to celebrate this joy with us."

Isaac strode around the table, put his arm around Cadence, pulling her into an embrace.

She leaned into him, while he inhaled her scent, without hunter's block. He held her essence in his lungs, letting her aroma dwell in him, expanding his lungs painfully, but at the same time filling his heart in a way it had never been.

KEEP READING for an excerpt from the next Shifters Forever Worlds book!

Book 3 of Shifters Forever After: A spin off series of Shifters Forever.

Polar bear shifter Jonah Romanoff's got one goal. Be the best agent he can be in the Paranormal Unit of InterForce.

He didn't expect his ex to show up, prying into his secrets, opening up a can of worms, and throwing his bear and his heart into pandemonium.

Curvy falcon shifter Fiona hasn't told him the truth about why she broke it off. Now she has to figure out why he's lying to her.

Except the secrets don't seem to matter as much when the motivation becomes saving the life of the one you love.

CHAPTER 1

This was a bad fucking idea.

The epic fail of bad ideas. Accepting Miriam Romanoff's invitation to join the Romanoffs for Christmas dinner would go down in Fiona Forester's history as the most epically stupid thing she'd done.

Who accepts to have dinner at the home of her ex's family?

Falcon shifter Fiona fiddled with the silverware Miriam had set out.

Me. Total idiot. Me. Totally.

It wasn't a big damned surprise that Jonah wasn't here. *One of his brothers must have told him I'd be here.*

Fiona looked at Ky—Malachi Romanoff. Ky had his hand on his mate's stomach and was beaming a smile about her pregnancy. They'd just announced Laken would be having his baby.

Was it Ky who told? Or Isaac? She turned her glance to the other Romanoff brother. Isaac was all google-eyed about his new mate, Cadence Araya, Laken's sister.

Neither Ky nor Isaac looked particularly guilty. Why would they? They wouldn't feel bad about warning Jonah. Of course, they'd take their brother's side on this matter. She couldn't blame them for that.

Fiona glanced at Mikhail Romanoff, the boys' uncle. Maybe he spilled the beans. Mikhail had raised all three boys after they lost their parents. He probably wouldn't talk to her at all.

Ugh. Why did I accept Miriam's invitation?

Fiona glanced at Miriam, an arctic fox shifter, curvy, like all the rest of them, only with a few more curves, an easy smile, and a twinkle in her eyes. She caught Fiona watching her. The smile broadened and she gave a little nod, almost as if she were saying that Fiona shouldn't worry, that Jonah's absence had nothing to do with her.

Yeah, right.

A knock at the door made everyone quiet down. Heads turned. In Fiona's stomach a knot took root. She shook it off. There was no reason to fret. That wasn't Jonah. She didn't sense his polar bear. Her falcon would surely have picked up his bear's presence.

Were they expecting someone else? They hadn't

said, but then again, it's not like Fiona was part of the planning committee.

Miriam excused herself and made for the door, with Mikhail close behind her, always ever mindful of his mate. Fiona had known the Romanoffs for years. She'd always admired the way Mikhail cared for his mate. She hoped she could have the same one day.

You had that with Jonah, her falcon reminded her.

And you know why that didn't work, she reminded her falcon back.

She studied her fork to keep from having to look at his brothers and their questioning glances. She knew she didn't belong here.

They'd had this discussion too many times in the years since she and Jonah had parted ways. Her falcon knew damned well there was nothing that could be done about the matter. It was for Jonah's own good.

She dropped the fork on the plate, it clattered loudly, but not loudly enough to drown out that voice.

Jonah.

His voice. God. He still did it for her. Just hearing one sentence had made her body react. A flood, a tightening, a pulse that throbbed at her core.

Goddamn him. And I couldn't even tell what the hell he just said.

Yup, that was the effect that damned sexy ass polar bear shifter had on her.

Still.

Years later.

Damn, already.

You'd think she'd have gotten over him. Replaced him.

The only thing she'd replaced him with was in her nightstand drawer and ran on batteries. And that was a damned sorry excuse for a replacement, but it beat the hell out of having to fake interest in another man. There was no way in hell another man could make her feel the things he had.

Her falcon screeched in her mind, the shrieking made Fiona want to cover her ears, but she knew that wouldn't do any good. The sound was in her mind.

Stop. Please. Stop.

The falcon kept up the high-pitched vocalizations.

I can't understand anything you're saying. Stop!

Jonah Romanoff followed his aunt and uncle into the dining room.

"I'm sorry I'm late. It's a case. Kept me busy."

"On Christmas day?" Aunt Miriam frowned. "It's a holiday. A federal holiday."

"Criminals don't take a holiday, Miriam." Uncle Mikhail kissed her on the cheek. "I'm starving. Let's eat."

"Me t—" Jonah froze.

No. It couldn't be.

Fiona Forester.

Here.

Here to fuck my life up. As if it's not fucked up enough.

He clenched his jaw, fought the urge to make tight fists and drive them through the wall.

He wished he could scent her. He wished he could have known she was here in advance. He couldn't have.

He studied the woman who'd taken his heart ages ago. The woman he'd almost taken as his mate. The woman who still had his heart, except now it was in shambles—a desolate barren environment where nothing grew.

His broken heart was one thing, but his cock sure as hell wasn't broken.

His loins burned with the need to be deep within her again. She was his mate. He mourned her. Her blond hair was pulled back, exposing the neck he used to love to kiss and nibble on. The neck that led to that spot near her shoulder where he'd almost couple-bonded her the night before she broke it off between them.

Her gaze was concentrated on the fork that had cracked the dinner plate. He didn't need preternatural shifter vision to see that she'd broken Aunt Miriam's fine china.

Fiona's eyes glistened, as if she were fighting tears,

those blue eyes he'd loved looking into, the blue eyes he'd gotten lost in so many times.

Not tears for me, that's for sure. She's the one who dumped me.

He nodded at her, though he knew his eyes were throwing lethal weapons.

Fiona looked down, her eyelashes casting shadows on her high cheekbones. Her expression sparked an emotion in him.

It took everything he had not to run to her, to take her into his arms, to claim her.

Instead he turned to his aunt. "You've been busy." He let his tone carry that it wasn't lost on him that she'd manipulated the situation to have Fiona here. Oh, yeah, he blamed his aunt for this for sure.

And of course, it figures that of all the people in the world, the one who knows me best would be here...

...at a time like this.

The worst time of all.

Ever.

What's next?

Motivation

Another book of the Shifters Forever Worlds, a place teeming with shifters!

Please refer to the website for newest releases as we spend time with our Shifters Forever and all the wonderful spin off series!

ElleThorne.com

Thank you for reading!

SHIFTERS FOREVER SERIES

Are you ready for it?

I have a whole world full of shifters to share with you.

I'm listing them here, in the suggested reading order, though I've tried to make it so that you can pick up anywhere in the series as we all have probably done that at one point or another.

Many of these are organized in box sets for savings. Be sure to visit www.ellethorne.com to see which box sets are out!

Where's the best place to start? Well, probably with SHIFTERS FOREVER.

SHIFTERS FOREVER

Grizzly bear shifters and their mates steam up the pages in these swoon-worthy paranormal romances. From trespassers with hidden agendas to curvaceous women who are ready to take a chance, the stories in this collection will capture your heart.

- PROTECTION
- SEDUCTION
- PERSUASION
- INVITATION
- TEMPTATION
- ATTRACTION

ALWAYS AFTER DARK

A spinoff with the white tiger from Shifters Forever: Vax, born Vittorio Tiero. He's the one that helped Kane out during a shifter battle. Follow the Tiero family, a group of white tiger shifters, as they head to America to find love... and heart-stopping danger. Full of romance, suspense, and gritty drama, this red-hot collection is sure to entertain!

- CONTROVERSY
- TERRITORY
- ADVERSARY
- SANCTUARY

NEVER AFTER DARK

Another spinoff that takes place in Europe. Here we visit cities along the Mediterranean and meet the old school Tiero white tiger shifters who are resistant to change.

- FORBIDDEN
- FORSAKEN
- FORGOTTEN
- FOREPLAY

ONLY AFTER DARK

Taking place in New Orleans, the Arceneaux shifters, led by Lézare, Vax's white tiger cousin—on his mother's side—are sure to capture your hearts. The Arceneaux are the black sheep of the family. Lézare doesn't cave to public opinion. He dictates policy in the area he rules and he shuns old school European rules and regimes.

- DESIRABLE
- INSATIABLE
- COMBUSTIBLE
- UNDENIABLE
- INEVITABLE
- INESCAPABLE

BITTER FALLS FOREVER

This romance features Mae Forester's nephew Dane Forester, a freewheeling, sexy, successful, movie star who uses every role and every woman to escape and forget the heartbreak he left in Bitter Falls.

• UNBOUND

BARELY AFTER DARK

This series features more of Mae Forester's nephews! Grizzly bear shifters steam up the pages in these swoon-worthy paranormal romances. From trespassers with hidden agendas to curvaceous women who are ready to take a chance, the stories in this collection will capture your heart.

• CROSS
• LANCE
• JUDGE

EVER AFTER DARK

Get ready to be introduced to the white tigers you learned to love in Always After Dark, Never After Dark, and Only After Dark. See their heritage. Visit

Giovanni Tiero and his brothers Federico and Tito. Get reacquainted with Isabel Tiero and meet her sister Capriana Valenti.

- STONEBOUND
- FORMIDABLE

SHIFTERS FOREVER AFTER

This series follows a group of polar bears in New York. Russian and rumored to be mobbed up, they are a powerhouse of shifters, determining the fate of many on the East Coast. Mikhail Romanoff, Layla's father, runs this outfit with an iron fist. Layla's sexy cousin Malachi features prominently in this series.

- COMPLICATION
- FASCINATION
- MOTIVATION
- CAPTIVATION
- FLIRTATION
- INFATUATION

FOREVER AFTER DARK

A series which takes place in Denver, Colorado. Enter a world of secrets and forbidden love. Panther shifters who who share their worlds with elementals must decide who they can trust—and who they can't live without.

- Notorious
- Scandalous
- Delicious
- Perilous

SHIFTERS FOREVER MORE Grizzly bear shifters, dragon shifters, sorceresses, elementals, and all types of other paranormal beings and their mates steam up the pages as the Bear Canyon Valley clan sorts through trespassers with hidden agenda, hidden military compounds, top secret experiments and curvaceous women who are ready to take a chance. The romances in this collection will capture your heart and leave your head spinning!

- Confusion
- Decision
- Possession
- Illusion
- Passion
- Impression

FINALLY AFTER DARK

Follow a pack of dire wolves as they encounter Valkyrie and Berserkers and determine the origins of their kind throughout the ages, while discovering their fated mates.

- ORIGINS
- CHALLENGE
- DAMAGE
- RAVAGE
- MORE TO FOLLOW!

I do hope you'll be able to join me on this wonderful journey with our Shifters Forever Worlds Shifters and their mates!

To receive exclusive updates from Elle Thorne and to be the first to get your hands on the next release, please sign up for her mailing list.

Elle Thorne Newsletter

If you can't click, just put this in your browser: http://www.ellethorne.com/contact

MY PERSONAL GUARANTEE:

THIS WILL ONLY BE USED TO ANNOUNCE NEW RELEASES AND SPECIALS. AND TO GIVE MY WONDERFUL SPECIAL READERS A LITTLE GIFT.

SHIFTERS REALMS

I have another new world of shifters! How exciting! I can't wait to share them with you!

Be sure to visit www.ellethorne.com to see which ones are out!

Where's the best place to start? Here we go!

IRON FLATS

Wolf shifters and their mates steam up the pages in these paranormal romances. From rovers with hidden agendas to women who are ready to take a chance, to unknown the stories in this collection will capture your heart.

- IRON FLATS EXILE
- IRON FLATS JUSTICE
- IRON FLATS REBEL
- IRON FLATS MAVERICK

MORE TO FOLLOW!

I do hope you'll be able to join me on this wonderful journey with our Shifters Forever Worlds Shifters and their mates!

To receive exclusive updates from Elle Thorne and to be the first to get your hands on the next release, please sign up for her mailing list.

Elle Thorne Newsletter

If you can't click, just put this in your browser: http://www.ellethorne.com/contact

MY PERSONAL GUARANTEE:
THIS WILL ONLY BE USED TO ANNOUNCE NEW RELEASES AND SPECIALS. AND TO GIVE MY WONDERFUL SPECIAL READERS A LITTLE GIFT.

Shifters Forever Worlds

Shifter Realms

For sales and news, sign up for the newsletter! Thank you for purchasing and downloading my book. Words can't express what it means to me. If you enjoyed this read, please remember to take a second to leave a review. I'd love to know what your favorite parts were.

The fun isn't about to stop. Make sure you sign up for the link to the newsletter.

Hearing from you means the world to me. This would not be possible without you and your love for reading.

With much gratitude, I thank you!

It took Elle Thorne years to stop being a closet romantic.

Originally from Europe, she wouldn't dream of living anywhere else but Texas. Unless it was another southern—translation: warm!—state. A southern European by birth, she wants to be near the water and the Mediterranean temperatures if possible.

Where does she like to hang out? Near a lake, a beach, preferably with a latte—extra shot of espresso, please! She's inspired by the everyday men who make dreams come true. She loves a roughneck, especially one with a callous or two on his hands. A man who knows how to fix a car, please a woman, and protect what's his.

Nothing less will do.

To receive exclusive updates from Elle Thorne and to be the first to get your hands on the next release, please sign up for her mailing list.
Put this in your browser:
www.ellethorne.com/contact

MY PERSONAL GUARANTEE:
THIS WILL ONLY BE USED TO ANNOUNCE NEW RELEASES AND SPECIALS. AND TO GIVE MY WONDERFUL SPECIAL READERS A LITTLE GIFT.